Bless

THE LORD

OH MY SOUL

Psalm 10:3

Sam, The Visionary Kid and Al the Fugitive

Merlinus Publishers
First Published 2025

Lytham, Lancashire, United Kingdom

For permission requests, contact

Graham Haynes
Email: grahamhaynes1@hotmail.com

Author Website
grahamhaynesauthor.co.uk

I WILL WALK BY
FAITH
EVEN
When
I CANNOT SEE

Dedicated

I Dedicate this book to my Daughter Nicola, a True Visionary and to my late wife Carole, now in the arms of Jesus. Her inspiration meant the world to me.

Isaiah 61:1-3

The Spirit of the Sovereign lord is on me, because the lord has anointed me to preach the good news to the poor, he has sent me to bind up the broken-hearted and proclaim freedom for the captives and release from darkness for the prisoners, to proclaim the year of the lord's favour and the day of vengeance of our God, to comfort all who mourn.

RISE UP
and
PRAY
LUKE 22:46

Chapters

Chapter Titles:	*Page*
Chapter One:	
Divine Encounters	9
Chapter Two:	
A Matter of Trust	13
Chapter Three:	
The Meeting With Pastor Peter...	36
Chapter Four:	
Back to the Canal	41
Chapter Five:	
A Pastor's Concern	55
Chapter Six:	
Operation Horton...	62
Chapter Seven:	
Confronting The Soothsayer...	79
Chapter Eight:	
Can You Hear That?...	109
Chapter Nine:	
Healing Hearts...	134
Chapter Ten:	
Solving The Mystery...	162

HAVE
patience
GOD ISN'T
finished
yet

Ephesians 1:11,

Before we were even born, he gave us our destiny, that we would fulfill the plan of God who always accomplishes every purpose and plan in is heart.

CHAPTER 1

DIVINE ENCOUNTERS

The November evening cast long shadows across the canal as Sam walked alone, his worn tennis shoes scuffing against the frost-kissed gravel. At twenty-four years old and standing 5'8" with a slender frame of eleven and a half stone, he wasn't someone who turned heads. His faded jeans hung loose on his waist, and his grey hoodie seemed a size too large, but comfort mattered more to Sam than appearance. He pulled the hoodie tighter against the damp chill that had settled over the waterway.

The canal stretched on before him like a dark ribbon, its surface reflecting the first stars of evening surrounding the bright North Star in a cluster. Bare branches of towering willows drooped over the water, their leaves long since dropped in the autumn season. The towpath itself was muddy at the edges, though still firm enough in the center for walking. The water moved sluggishly, carrying scattered leaves and the occasional plastic bottle toward the distant locks.

The evening air carried the familiar scent of approaching winter, but Sam's attention was drawn to the shadows beneath the canal bridge. There, huddled in sleeping bags and cardboard boxes, were the faces of those society had forgotten. His heart clenched as he recognized how close he'd come to joining them just a few years ago. The memory of his darkest days flooded back, - the needle marks that had once dotted his arms, now faded but still visible if you knew where to look. His parents, both in their sixties when they'd taken him back in, had never given up on him. Their home had become his sanctuary, the safe walls he needed to rebuild his life. But now they were gone, taken within weeks of each other by COVID-19 just three months ago. The house had been sold to cover their medical expenses, leaving Sam truly alone for the first time in his life.

He touched the small cross in his pocket - his mother's last gift to him.

"I know you'll find your way," she'd whispered through the hospital room window, her voice barely audible through the phone. "God has special plans for you, Samuel." Those were her last words to him.

That's when it happened. Standing there on the towpath, Sam felt it - a presence so profound it nearly brought him to his knees. Divine love washed over him like warm summer rain, and the North Star seemed to pulse with newfound brilliance through a break in the clouds. Tears welled in his eyes as understanding dawned - this was his calling. God was speaking to him, showing him his purpose.

"I hear you," he whispered to the sky, his voice trembling. "But where do I start?"

As if in answer, footsteps approached from behind. Sam turned to see a tall, lean man in his forties wearing a three-quarter-length raincoat, his breath visible in the cold air. There was something both commanding and humble about his presence.

"Who are you?" Sam asked, surprised by his boldness.

The stranger's eyes held a depth of understanding that put Sam at ease. "I'm Al," he said simply. "Some call me the Fugitive. But I perfer just Al." He gestured to a nearby log. "Mind if we talk?"

As they settled onto the damp log, their breath mingling in the cold air, Al explained his story - how his family and friends claimed to search for him but never truly wanted to find him. His words resonated with Sam's journey of isolation and seeking.

"I was a lay pastor once," Al revealed, his voice softening. "But I lost my way.

Something about you called to me - I've been following you, watching how you interact with others, how you observe everything with such care. There's a light in you that reminds me of when I first heard the calling."

After Sam introduced himself, he felt compelled to share his own story, the drugs, the depression, losing his parents, and then the sudden moment of divine intervention just minutes ago. As he spoke, Al's eyes widened with recognition, and he reached out to squeeze Sam's shoulder, a gesture so paternal it brought fresh tears to Sam's eyes.

"You've been touched by His grace," Al said, his voice filled with wonder. "I haven't felt His presence so strongly since..." he paused, emotion catching in his throat. "Would you let me baptize you? Right here in the canal?"

Despite the November chill and the dark water, Sam didn't hesitate. This was what his mother had meant about God's plans. They made their way to the water's edge, where Al gently guided Sam into the canal. The cold hit him like a physical blow, but Sam barely noticed.

"In the name of the Father, the Son, and the Holy Spirit," Al's voice rang out as he lowered Sam into the water. When Sam emerged, gasping and grinning, both men were crying, not from the cold, but from the pure joy of a divine connection.

"This is what I'm meant to do," Al explained as they sat on the log again.

"Being a lay Pastor means taking Christ's message to those who need it most. I've seen miracles, Sam, addicts finding salvation, the homeless discovering purpose. God didn't just bring us together - He orchestrated this whole moment. Your newfound connection with Him, my wandering here, even the North Star breaking through the clouds just now."

As the evening grew darker, they noticed an older man approaching them on the towpath. He moved with an uncertain step, his clothes well-worn but clean.

"Hello," he called out. "I'm Soapy - that's what folks around here call me anyway. I couldn't help but notice you two seem... different. Like you might understand."

Sam and Al exchanged knowing looks. Their journey was about to begin.

Worry ends
WHEN FAITH
in god begins

Ephesians 4:28.

Anyone who has been stealing must. Steal no longer but must work, doing something useful with their hands, that they may have something to share with those in need.

CHAPTER 2

A MATTER OF TRUST

There's something I need to tell you both," Soapy said, his weathered face creasing with concern. "My church - well, our church now if you're willing, we're facing a situation that needs... special attention. The kind that requires people who can see things others might miss." He glanced over meaningfully at Sam. "Pastor Peter, he's a good man, but he's at his wit's end with this one."

Al studied Soapy's face in the gathering darkness. "What kind of situation?"

"Best if Pastor Peter explains it himself," Soapy replied, wringing his hands. Will you come with me? The church isn't far."

Sam felt a gentle nudge in his spirit. "How far?" he asked, still dripping from his baptism in the canal.

"Just through those trees," Soapy pointed to a spire ahead. "You can see the spire from here."

A few minutes later Sam, Al and Soapy arrived at the Church gates.

"Here we are," Soapy said softly, gesturing to the small stone church ahead. His weathered face creased with worry. "I know this might seem strange, bringing you here right after your baptism, but..." He hesitated, searching for words. "Something has happened. Something that's shaken our whole congregation. When I saw you by the canal, I sensed God was working through you both, and I knew then..."

"That God had led us here," Sam finished, understanding dawning in his eyes. He looked up at the North Star, it seemed to pulse brighter above the church spire and he placed a gentle hand on Soapy's shoulder. "Tell us more. We want to help."

Soapy cleared his throat and began to explain. "Last week a precious prayer bowl went missing. It was stolen! But this is not just about it being taken that has shocked us all here; especially Pastor Peter," Soapy told them, his voice tight with emotion. "It's about trust. Faith. When something sacred is violated..." He shook his head. "But Pastor Peter will explain everything."

The heavy wooden doors creaked open, and Sam felt it immediately, a presence so powerful it made his knees weak. The aisle stretched on before them, light from the stained-glass windows painting jewelled patterns across worn stone floors. Brass candlesticks gleamed softly in the evening light, and the air itself seemed charged with centuries of prayers.

Al watched in amazement as Sam's entire demeanour transformed. The uncertain young man he'd baptized hours ago now stood straighter; his face illuminated with inner light. "Sam?" he whispered.

"I can feel Him here," Sam whispered back, his voice thick with emotion. "So strongly, Al. Like... like my parents are here too, somehow. With Him in His presence."

"Ah, Soapy! Who are your friends?" A warm voice echoed from the chancel.

Pastor Peter emerged a stocky man in his fifties with kind eyes and flour on his sleeve. "Welcome, welcome! Though I must say, you both look like you've had quite a journey."

Soapy stepped forward. "Pastor, this is Sam and Al. They're... well, they're exactly who we need right now. I met them down by the canal. Sam has a gift for seeing what others miss, and Al..." He glanced at his new friend. "Al understands people's hearts. They have come to help us with our situation."

Peter studied them thoughtfully. "You've been walking the towpath all day?"

At their nods, his pastoral instincts took over.

"Then our troubles can wait until morning. You need rest, food, warmth. The rectory has spare rooms, and Mrs. Chambers always leaves soup simmering."

"But-" Sam began to protest.

"God's work is better done with a clear head and rested body," Peter said firmly. "Have breakfast with me tomorrow, and we'll discuss everything then."

The next morning dawned clear and cold. Sam woke early, his mind already turning over the mystery that awaited them. He found Al in the kitchen, deep in conversation with Pastor Peter and Soapy over steaming mugs of tea.

"Ah, Sam!" Al's face brightened. "I was just telling Peter about your insight with the homeless under the bridge. The way you recognized God's calling."

Sam greeted everyone warmly as he sat down at the table. Pastor Peter's hands trembled slightly as he placed his teacup on the rectory table. Morning light streamed through the window, catching the dust motes in its beam. Sam, Al, and Soapy waited in respectful silence as the pastor gathered his thoughts.

"A week ago," Peter began, his voice heavy with grief, "our bronze bowl just vanished. Not just any bowl, you understand. This was our prayer bowl, centuries old, passed down through generations of faithful servants." He paused, swallowing hard. "At first, we thought someone had moved it for cleaning, or perhaps relocated it for safekeeping. But as days passed..."

"When did you last see it, Pastor?" Sam asked gently, leaning forward.

"Sunday service. It was there throughout the morning, catching the light just as it always has." Peter's eyes grew distant. "Joan Baker, she is with God now, but she always used to say it looked like it held liquid sunshine."

Al shifted in his chair. "You've asked everyone who was present about it?"

"Yes, there were ten of us here at the time," Peter nodded, counting on his fingers. "All longstanding members of our congregation. Good people, faithful people. I can't imagine any of them..." His voice trailed off.

Sam closed his eyes briefly, sensing divine guidance. "Sometimes good people lose their way, Pastor. Especially when they're hurting."

"What exactly are you suggesting?" Soapy asked, his brow furrowed.

"We need to look at this deeper than just the physical disappearance," Sam explained. "The bowl isn't just valuable in monetary terms, is it? It holds special memories, connections."

"Joan's husband," Peter murmured "It's true, Arthur hasn't been the same since she passed. The bowl was special to her."

Sensing divine guidance, Sam knew what they had to do. "Let us speak with each person who was here that day. Not as investigators, but as brothers and sisters in Christ. Sometimes people need a safe space to unburden their hearts."

"You think someone will confess?" Peter asked, hope flickering in his eyes.

"I think God led us here for a reason," he replied. "This isn't just about finding a missing bowl. It's about healing whatever wound led to its taking."

Soapy began writing names on a piece of paper. "The Fields were here, and the Oswald's. Arthur Baker, of course. The Francis sisters..."

"We'll need to approach this carefully," Al cautioned. "Trust, once broken, needs gentle hands to mend."

"And what if..." Peter hesitated, "what if we discover something we'd rather not know?"

Sam reached across the table and squeezed the pastor's hand. "Then we'll remember that God's grace is bigger than any human failing. This community is strong enough to weather truth with love."

"Even if it's someone we trust?" Soapy asked quietly.

"Especially then," Sam answered. "Because that's when they'll need us most."

Sam sat silent for a long moment; eyes closed in prayer. The morning light painted shaded patterns on the rectory table as the others waited, respecting his communion with the divine. Finally, he opened his eyes, clarity evident in his expression. "The Holy Spirit works through personal connection," he said, remembering how his parents had helped him, gave him shelter and made him face his demons. "Sometimes people just need to know they're safe to speak the truth."

"I'll make the calls," Peter said, rising from his chair. "Arrange times that work for everyone. Soapy, would you help me? You know their schedules better than I do."

While they waited, Al studied his young friend's face. "You're sensing something specific, aren't you?"

"Not yet," Sam replied, absently touching the cross in his pocket. "But I feel God's guidance. Like when we met by the canal, God is aligning everything for a purpose."

When Peter and Soapy returned thirty minutes later, they carried not just a list of names and addresses, but a carefully planned schedule. Sam accepted the paper, noting the neat organization, times, locations, even small notes about each family.

"Soapy should go with you," Peter suggested, gesturing to his friend. "He knows every street and alley in the parish, and more importantly, he knows the people. They trust him."

Sam glanced at Soapy's weathered, kind face. "Would you be willing? We do need you to introduce us."

"Of course," Soapy replied warmly. "These people are my family. If one of them is hurting enough to do this..." He shook his head. "Then I'll be there to help."

The November morning shimmered brightly as they approached the Fields Victorian terrace. Pink and yellow roses, remarkably resilient against the heavy autumn chill, climbed trellises on either side of the front door. Through a set of delicate lace curtains, they could see the warm glow of table lamps.

"The Fields have been with us forty years," Soapy whispered as they waited. "Their daughter was married in our church last spring."

Margaret Field opened the door before they could knock as if she'd been watching for them. Her silver hair was neatly pinned back, and she wore the kind of floral apron that spoke of fresh-baked comfort.

"Come in, come in," she urged, ushering them through to a sitting room that radiated decades of family life. Mr. Field, tall and scholarly in his cardigan, rose from his armchair. Photographs crowded every surface - children growing up, graduations, weddings, all captured in silver frames that Mrs. Field polished regularly. The air carried the lingering sweetness of baked bread and Earl Grey.

"Such a terrible business," Mrs. Field fretted, her hands trembling as she poured tea into her best china cups. "That bowl's seen so many baptisms, so many prayers. My grandmother used to tell me how it caught the light during morning service like it was filled with holy fire."

Sam accepted his cup with thanks, "Did anything seem unusual that Sunday?" he asked softly.

Mr. Field removed his glasses, polishing them with a handkerchief - a habit, Sam suspected, from his teaching days. "You know," he said slowly, "Arthur Baker wasn't himself. Distracted during the hymns and he usually sings so beautifully. Joan used to say his voice was what first drew her to him." He shook his head sadly. "He's not been the same since she passed, of course, but this was different somehow."

"Different how?" Sam prompted gently.

"Like he was carrying something heavy," Mrs. Field interjected, setting down a plate of still-warm scones. "Not just grief anymore, but... something else. Something darker."

Mr. Field nodded in agreement. "He kept looking over his shoulder during the service as if expecting someone. And when the bowl caught the morning light - well, I saw him wince. Actually wince, as if it hurt him to look at it. He also left and then when we were outside, we saw him come out of the church again. Rather baffling if you ask me but Marg here said he must have forgotten his bag and went back in for it."

Sam exchanged a meaningful glance with Al. The Fields' observations just confirmed what the Holy Spirit had been whispering to his heart. As they then prepared to leave, Mrs. Field pressed a paper bag of scones into Soapy's hands.

"For later," she insisted. "And please... help Arthur if you can. Joan would be heartbroken to see him struggling so."

Walking away from the Fields' warm home towards Arthur Baker's house, Sam felt the weight of divine purpose settling more firmly on his shoulders. The Fields weren't involved in the bowl's disappearance, but they'd provided something more valuable - a window into Arthur's troubled soul.

Arthur Baker's house stood in sharp contrast to the Fields' welcoming home. Heavy burgundy curtains blocked the morning light, casting the rooms in perpetual twilight. The front garden, once Joan's pride with its carefully tended roses, had surrendered to autumn's decay. Arthur himself seemed to have diminished since his wife's passing - his tall frame stooped, his clothes hanging loosely on his thinning body.

At sixty-five, Arthur's face bore the deep lines of recent grief, his silver hair unkempt where Joan would have once insisted on a proper trim. His hands, Sam noticed, couldn't keep still, constantly adjusting his collar, straightening already straight cushions, fingers drumming an anxious rhythm on his armchair.

"Please, sit," he gestured toward the faded floral sofa, his voice carrying a tension that seemed to vibrate through the stale air. Layers of dust danced in the thin shaft of light that escaped the curtains. "Have you... have you found anything out?"

Sam's eyes were drawn to the single photograph still hanging on the otherwise bare walls - Joan at their fortieth-anniversary celebration, her smile radiant as she stood beside the church's bronze bowl, next to it a vase filled with roses. The rest of the walls showed pale rectangles where other photos had once hung, like gaps in a smile.

"Tell me about that Sunday, Arthur. You went back for your bag?"

"Yes," Arthur's fingers resumed their nervous drumming a jerky beat against the worn fabric. "Left it in my usual pew." His pale blue eyes darted to the photograph. "Third from the back left side. Joan's favourite spot." His voice forced on her name, and he swallowed hard. "She loved that bronze bowl."

"And you saw the bowl when you left?" Sam kept his voice gentle, watching how Arthur's right foot began to tap against the carpet.

"Yes, yes," Arthur nodded too quickly, his collar suddenly seeming too tight as he tugged at it. "It was there, in its usual place. Catching the light, just as..." He trailed off, lost momentarily in memory.

"Were you the last to leave?" Sam pressed carefully.

Arthur's fingers moved from drumming to gripping his armchair. "Usually am, apart from Soapy. He locks up, you know." A bead of sweat appeared at his temple despite the room's chill.

"So Soapy left after you, and the bowl was still there?"

"Yes, that's right. Perfectly visible. Normal place." Arthur's answers were becoming abrupt, his eyes fixed on a point just over Sam's shoulder.

Al, who had been quietly observing, leaned forward. "Joan would have been able to see it clearly from her pew, wouldn't she?"

Arthur's composure cracked slightly, a tremor running through his hands. "Yes, she used to say it looked like it held God's light," he whispered.

Sam thanked Arthur and led the way out, noting how quickly Arthur closed the door behind them. As they walked toward the Oswalds' house, the early afternoon sun settling in, Al touched Sam's arm.

"Did you see how he couldn't look at Joan's photo when he talked about the bowl?"

Sam nodded gravely. "And how he kept saying 'usual place' - like he was trying to convince himself more than us."

The Oswald's Victorian semi-detached seemed to lean slightly under the weight of its literary contents. Books spilled from every available surface, creating precarious towers that defied gravity. Bernard Oswald, tall and lanky with wire-rimmed glasses perpetually sliding down his nose, threw open the door with characteristic enthusiasm.

"Ah! The investigating team!" he boomed, ushering them through a narrow canyon of encyclopaedias. "Mind the Chaucer on your left - first editions are rather temperamental."

The sitting room had surrendered to academia years ago. What might have once been a formal parlour now resembled a professor's study after a particularly vigorous research session. Martha Oswald, small and bird-like, perched in her armchair like a sparrow in a paper nest, surrounded by open books and yellow legal pads covered in her precise handwriting.

"Fascinating piece, that bowl," Bernard mused, clearing space on the sofa by relocating a stack of theological journals. "Pre-Reformation craftsmanship, you know. The engravings suggest Northumbrian influence - remarkable preservation considering the Dissolution period. Did you know it likely survived by being hidden in a priest's hole? The pattern of wear on the rim suggests-"

"Bernie," Martha interrupted fondly, "They're not here for a history lesson. Though," she added, her sharp eyes fixing on Sam, "you're feeling something about Arthur Baker, arn't you?"

Sam leaned forward. "What makes you say that?"

"We may be buried in books," Bernard said, suddenly serious, "but we do observe more than people think. That Sunday, Martha and I had to leave early for choir practice, but something felt... off."

"Off how?" Al prompted.

"Arthur was wearing his Sunday suit," Martha explained, "the one Joan bought him last Christmas. He never wears it normally, says it pains him too much. But that day..." She exchanged glances with her husband.

"He was dressed as if for an occasion," Bernard continued. "And there was that woman hovering near him - the new one."

"Jan," Martha added. "She's been attending for what, three months now? Always sitting just behind Arthur, always finding reasons to speak with him after service."

"Did you notice anything about the bowl that day?" Sam asked.

Bernard removed his glasses, polishing them thoughtfully. "Actually, yes. Usually, the light hits it during the third hymn. But that Sunday, someone had shifted it slightly. The angle was all wrong."

"By about fifteen degrees," Martha added precisely.

Thanking Bernard and Marther, the trio prepared to leave. Bernard pressed a small leather-bound book into Sam's hands.

"The church's original inventory records," he explained. "Including the first mention of the bowl in 1546. Perhaps... perhaps understanding its history might help understand its future."

Outside, autumn sunshine had given way to thick clouds.

"Back to Peter?" Soapy suggested. "Mrs. Chambers always does a proper Sunday roast, and we've learned more than I expected."

Sam nodded, Bernard's book heavy in his pocket. "We need to tell Peter about this woman Jan," he said quietly. "And about the bowl being moved. Someone wanted to make sure Arthur couldn't see that reflection."

"To make it easier?" Al questioned. "Or to prevent him from changing his mind?"

The church bells were striking 12 as they returned, the sound echoing across the grey afternoon. Inside, they found Pastor Peter in his study, surrounded by parish records and looking more worried than when they'd left.

"You've learned something," he said, not a question but a statement, looking up from his papers. The rich aroma of Mrs. Chambers' Sunday roast drifted in from the rectory kitchen.

Sam settled into a worn leather chair, Bernard's book still weighing in his pocket. "It's about Arthur," he began carefully. "And Jan."

Peter's face tightened. "I was afraid of that. What have you found?"

Al leaned against the bookshelf; his pastoral instincts engaged. "The bowl was moved that Sunday. Just enough to stop its reflection from reaching Joan's pew."

"Where Arthur still sits," Soapy added quietly.

"Martha Oswald noticed it first," Sam continued. "Bernard too. They said Arthur was wearing the suit Joan gave him, something he hasn't done since she passed."

"Like he was dressed for an occasion," Peter murmured, understanding dawning in his eyes.

"And Jan was there," Sam pressed on. "Sitting behind him, the Oswalds said. She always finds reasons to speak with him after service."

Peter rose suddenly, pacing to the window. "She asked about the bowl's history when she first arrived. She seemed particularly interested in its value." He turned back to them. "I thought she was just showing appreciation for our heritage."

"Or identifying a target," Al suggested gently. "And a vulnerable soul to manipulate."

"Arthur Baker left the church," Sam said slowly, each word weighted with significance as he sat in the comfortable chair. "He made a point of mentioning that Soapy locked up after him." Sam suddenly realised the obvious. "The bag was deliberate," he said quietly. "A reason to return. To pass by the bowl one more time when the church was nearly empty." His hand touched the cross in his pocket, seeking guidance. "He must have planned it carefully, the timing, the excuse, everything."

"But Arthur?" Peter's voice cracked slightly. "He and Joan practically built this congregation. Why would he...?"

"Sometimes," Al interjected gently, "the people closest to something are the most vulnerable to being used against it."

Sam nodded grimly. "We should confront him now. Before..."

"Wait." Peter held up his hand. "We've only interviewed half the congregation. What if we're missing something? Some piece that could help us understand - to help him?"

Silence fell as they considered this. Outside, the church bells chimed for afternoon prayers, their familiar sound carrying both comfort and urgency.

"You're right," Sam conceded. "We need to be thorough. Not just for the bowl's sake, but for Arthur's. Let's complete the other interviews first."

Mrs. Chambers appeared in the doorway, her face pink from the kitchen heat, wiping her hands with herapron.

"Dinner's ready, if you're done plotting."

Over roast beef and Yorkshire puddings, they shared every detail they'd gathered: the Fields' observations of Arthur's distraction, his nervous behaviour during their visit, the Oswalds' precise recollections.

"What troubles me most," Sam said, breaking apart a warm roll, "is how carefully this was orchestrated. Moving the bowl to block its reflection - that shows planning. Understanding of what might trigger Arthur's conscience."

"Like Joan's presence," Al nodded. "Arthur knows she's watching over him through that bowl."

"Then we will need to visit Arthur again," Peter decided. "But not just about the bowl. About what's truly been taken from him - his peace."

Sam touched the cross in his pocket, feeling that familiar divine guidance.

"Tomorrow, we will, after we've spoken to the others," he suggested. "Let's eat first and then gather for prayers. Something tells me we'll need God's wisdom for what's coming. Then after lunch, we can go and speak to the others starting with the Francis sisters."

They all nodded, the weight of their discovery settling over them like a heavy mantle. As they moved toward the kitchen, Sam felt divine reassurance, he knew they were on the right path.

The afternoon sun had warmed the streets as they approached the Francis sisters' terraced house. Even from the pavement, the scent of Caribbean spices and fresh-baked coconut bread wafted through the open windows, a stark contrast to the November chill.

Marg opened the door, her dark eyes bright with welcome. At thirty, she carried herself with the quiet dignity of an older soul, her nurse's scrubs exchanged for a colourful dress that seemed to bring summer into the hallway.

"Come in, come in," she urged, leading them into a sitting room that could have been transported directly from Kingston. Bright fabrics draped the windows, and photographs of Jamaica lined the walls, beaches, mountains, and family gatherings competing for space with crucifixes and biblical verses painted in vibrant colours.

Marg's sister emerged from the kitchen, carrying a tray laden with tea and what looked like homemade ginger cake.

"I'm Constance," she said, setting down her burden, "but Mama named me Coolness after I brought peace to a family argument the day I was born." Her laugh was musical and infectious. "At least, that's how she tells it."

"The church has been blessed since they arrived," Soapy whispered to Sam. "Five years ago, straight from Kingston. They've brought so much life to our congregation."

"We know why you're here," Marg said, passing out teacups with efficiency that spoke of her nursing background. "About the bowl. It's been hard to think of anything else this week."

Sam accepted his tea gratefully. "Did you notice anything that Sunday?"

Coolness and Marg exchanged glances.

"We were watching Arthur," Coolness admitted. "We always do, since Joan passed. Back home, we believe the recently widowed need extra eyes watching over them."

"He was crying during 'Amazing Grace,'" Marg added softly. "Joan's favourite hymn. But it wasn't just grief this time. There was something else..."

"Fear," Coolness added. "Like when my little brother knew he was about to do something wrong but couldn't stop himself."

"And Jan?" Sam prompted.

"That woman," Marg's voice carried an edge now. "She's been hovering around Arthur like a John Crow - sorry, what you'd call a vulture. Always whispering, always touching his arm after service."

"Last Sunday," Coolness leaned forward, her voice dropping, "I saw her looking at the bowl during communion. Not like she was admiring it. Like she was..." she searched for the word.

"Measuring it," Marg finished. "And Arthur kept looking between her and Joan's empty pew. Like he was asking forgiveness for something."

As they prepared to leave, Coolness pressed a package of coconut bread into Soapy's hands. "For later," she said. "And Sam?" Her eyes held his. "When you find the bowl - and I know you will - remember that sometimes people do wrong things for what they think are right reasons."

Walking away, the sweet bread's aroma following them, Al touched Sam's arm. "They saw what many missed," he said quietly. "Not just what happened, but why."

"God's eyes and ears," Sam nodded. "Now we know it's not just about Arthur. It's about saving him from whatever hold Jan has on him."

Next on their list was Mr & Mrs Dunkley. They lived in a meticulously maintained 1930s semi-detached, its red brick gleaming as if recently scrubbed. The garden path wound through precisely trimmed borders where the last roses of autumn made their final stand. Before they could reach the brass knocker, they saw Bert Dunkley's familiar figure in the doorway, his ex-military bearing evident even in casual clothes.

"Welcome, guys!" Bert's voice carried the cheerful authority of a retired headmaster. "Nice to see you. We've been expecting you." He ushered them along the hallway, its walls lined with photographs of school cricket teams and military reunions. "Please, come through and sit yourselves down."

The sitting room spoke of Olivia's touch - family portraits arranged with loving precision, and a collection of Toby jugs watching from glass-fronted cabinets. Olivia herself, small and slim with perfectly set silver hair, was arranging tea things on a tray.

"How can my husband and I help with this missing artefact, dear friends?" she asked, her hands hovering over the china cups like a conductor before an orchestra. "Such a dreadful business. I was just saying to Bert this morning, wasn't I, dear?"

"Indeed you were, Liv," Bert agreed, settling into his armchair with military precision. "Haven't seen the congregation this unsettled since the great hymn book debate of '98."

Sam accepted a cup of tea, - gratefully, all the talking was making him quite thirsty. "It's just to tie up a few loose ends," he said carefully. "When you left church last Sunday, Bert, did you see the bowl in its normal place?"

Bert straightened as if reporting to a superior officer. "Yes, absolutely. The bowl was exactly where it should be. Wouldn't have dared be otherwise - Joan

Baker would have had words, God rest her soul."

"Bert," Olivia chided gently, passing around a plate of perfectly arranged digestive biscuits, "we're not to speak ill of the departed."

"Not ill-speaking, my dear. Simple fact. That woman kept us all in line, didn't she? Church hasn't been the same since..." He trailed off, a shadow crossing his face. "Though I must say that new woman, Jan - something about her sets my teeth on edge. Military instinct, you know."

Sam exchanged a quick glance with Al. "How so?"

"Can't put my finger on it," Bert mused, absently adjusting his regimental tie pin. "But thirty years in the service teaches you to spot someone with ulterior motives. The way she watches everything like she's planning a campaign."

"Always sitting behind poor Arthur, fussing over him, smiling in his direction. It's all so false if you ask me." Olivia added, refreshing their cups with practiced grace. "Reminds me of when the girls at school would target the newly widowed professors. Not that I'm suggesting..." She flushed slightly.

"Thank you both," Sam said, rising. "You've been very helpful."

"Glad to help," Bert replied, standing at attention. "Just... find it quickly, won't you? For our community's sake. All this suspicion is not healthy."

As they walked back down the immaculate garden path, Sam mulled over the Dunkleys' observations. "Even they've noticed Jan's influence," he said quietly. "And they're right - she is running this like a military campaign."

"With poor Arthur as the unwitting soldier," Al added grimly. "The question is, what's her ultimate objective?"

The November afternoon was fading into evening as they approached Ryder Clifton's cottage. Unlike the other well-maintained homes they'd visited, Ryder's place had a bachelor's casual maintenance to the gardening - nature largely left to its own devices, apart from a carefully tended patch of vegetables in one corner.

Soapy stepped forward to knock, his weariness evident in his slightly stooped shoulders. After the many interviews, they were all feeling the weight of the day. The door opened to reveal Ryder Clifton, forty-something and dressed in paint-splattered overalls that suggested they'd interrupted his latest

DIY project.

"Come in, come in," he gestured, leading them through a narrow hallway where half-finished paintings leaned against the walls.

The sitting room reflected Ryder's artistic temperament - easels in corners, sketches pinned everywhere, and a view through the window that would have inspired any painter.

Al sank into an offered chair with visible relief. "Yawnnnnn. I feel a bit whacked with all this walking," he admitted, stretching his tired legs.

"I know," Sam sympathized, his own feet aching. "It's been a trying day, but here we are at Ryder's house now. He's the last one on the list so it won't take long."

Ryder cleared a stack of art magazines from a chair.

"I've been expecting you lot. Word travels fast in our little congregation." He ran a hand through his dishevelled hair. "That bowl - it's featured in quite a few of my sketches, you know. I loved painting it with its amazing light reflections."

"We just wanted to ask you about last Sunday," Sam said, noticing a half finished painting of the church interior where the bowl's bronze surface had been rendered in loving detail. "When you left the church, can you recall whether it was in its usual place?"

"Actually, I can," Ryder said, moving to the window as if the view might jog his memory further. "I gave it a particular look that day, I've been planning to use it in a new piece." He gestured to a blank canvas on an easel. "It was catching the light just so, though..." He frowned. "Something was different about the angle. Can't put my finger on exactly what."

"Different how?" Sam pressed gently.

"Well," Ryder turned back to them, his artist's eye evident in his precise observation, "usually it reflects light onto Joan's old pew, used to drive Arthur mad during sermons, but Joan loved it." He shook his head. "But that Sunday, the reflection was hitting the back wall instead. Thought it was odd, but figured someone had cleaned it and put it back slightly wrong.

Sam exchanged meaningful glances with his companions. Even Ryder was confirming their suspicions about Arthur and Jan's careful preparations.

"Thanks, Ryder," Sam said, rising despite his tiredness. "You've been a great help."

"Just find it, yeah?" Ryder called after them as they headed for the door. "That bowl's been part of more paintings than I can count. Church doesn't look right without it."

As they walked back toward the church through the gathering dusk, the North Star beginning to shine above them, Al voiced what they were all thinking.

"Every single person has mentioned Joan in some way. The bowl wasn't just part of the church - it was part of her legacy."

"Which makes its theft even more painful," Sam agreed quietly. "And makes Arthur's involvement even more tragic."

Twilight had settled over the church as they returned, casting long shadows through the stained-glass windows. They found Pastor Peter in the sitting room, silhouetted against the fading light as he returned a leather-bound volume to its shelf. The worn carpet muffled their footsteps, but something in the air made him turn even before they spoke.

"Hi, Pastor," they said in unison, their voices carrying the weariness of a long day's investigations.

Peter's face creased with concern as he studied their expressions. "So, have you finished all the interviews?"

"Yes, all done," Sam confirmed, sinking into a familiar armchair. His hand gently touched the cross in his pocket, seeking guidance for what must come next.

Soapy, ever practical, walked toward the kitchen. "I'll make some tea and put out a few biscuits. We need clear heads to review what we've learned." The familiar sounds of kettle and china provided a comforting backdrop to their mounting tension.

"Just what I need, relaxing with a cuppa," Al sighed with relief as Soapy returned bearing a laden tea tray. The rich aroma of Yorkshire Tea filled the room, grounding them in this moment of revelation.

Sam waited until they each had drank their tea before beginning.

"Each person we interviewed saw the bowl in its place that morning," he said carefully. "But they saw more than that. The Oswalds noticed it had been moved. Ryder Clifton confirmed it. The Francis sisters saw Arthur's distress during the hymns. The Dunkleys observed Jan's... influence."

"And then there's Arthur's return for his bag," Al added softly. "A careful plan, wouldn't you say?"

A heavy silence fell, broken only by the distant toll of evening bells. Peter set his cup down with a slight tremor. "We need to look deeper into Arthur's situation," he said finally. "There must be something powerful influencing him."

"The Holy Spirit has been guiding us," Sam said, his voice gaining strength. "2nd Timothy 2:26 speaks of the devil's trap - '*and that they will come to their senses and escape from the trap of the devil, who has taken them captive to do his will.*' If Arthur's caught in such a snare. God will reveal it..."

"Jan." Peter spoke the name like a revelation. "Always seeming so interested in our church's heritage... always finding reasons to speak with Arthur..."

"A dark influencer," Sam nodded grimly. "Tomorrow's work will need more than just questions and answers. We'll need God's strength to free Arthur from whatever hold she has on him."

Al straightened in his chair; his pastoral experience evident in his voice. "We'll need the whole armour of God - truth as a belt, righteousness as a breastplate, and our feet fitted with the readiness that comes from the gospel of peace."

They all nodded in solemn agreement. As evening deepened into night, they shared a simple meal, the television's muted glow providing background comfort. But their minds were already turned toward tomorrow's confrontation, each man silently praying for wisdom and strength. When Peter finally bid them goodnight, the North Star was shining brightly through the study window - a beacon of hope in the gathering darkness.

The morning mist still clung to the streets as they set out for Arthur's house, the North Star fading in the pale dawn light, though Sam could still feel its guidance. The early hour left the pavements empty except for a few cats slinking between garden gates and the occasional screech of milk floats making their rounds.

Soapy pulled his worn cardigan tighter against the morning chill, his breath visible in the cold air. "I hope things go well," he murmured, rubbing his weathered hands together. "But I can't stop feeling something isn't right."

"And you think worrying will help?" Al's voice carried warmth despite the morning chill. He placed a reassuring hand on Soapy's shoulder. "Remember what the Good Book says about anxiety?"

"Cast all your cares upon Him," Sam quoted softly, "for He cares for you."

"Exactly!" Al's voice carried the confidence of years in ministry. "We are all of one accord here. Everything will work out according to His plan."

"Still," Soapy persisted, "Arthur's been like family to us all. To think that Jan might have..."

"Look, over there!" Sam interrupted quietly, nodding ahead.

Through the thinning mist, twenty meters down the street, a man in a scuffed leather jacket paced like a caged animal. His movements carried a predatory grace that Sam recognized from his own days on the streets, the watchful tension of someone keeping lookout.

"Third time he's checked his watch in the last minute," Al observed.

"And the way he keeps looking at his phone," Sam added. "He's waiting for a signal."

A movement caught their attention - a neighbour at her garden gate, middle aged with kind eyes and worry lines etched deep. In her hands she clutched a gardening trowel though nothing needed tending in the November chill.

Sam approached her, "Excuse me, young lady. I hope you don't mind me asking, do you know that gentleman?" He gestured subtly toward the pacing man. A brief smile touched her lips at the courteous address before concern flooded back.

"Thank you for the 'young lady,' at my age, that's quite the compliment." She glanced nervously at the man in the leather jacket. "I don't know him, but I've seen him with that woman, Jan. She went into Arthur's house about twenty minutes ago. Been coming round more and more lately." Her voice dropped to a whisper. "That man always stays outside, watching. Like he is now. Sometimes they argue in the street, nothing I can quite hear, but their gestures..." She shook her head, then studied Sam's face intently. "You know Arthur?"

"We're friends," Sam assured her, noting how her shoulders relaxed slightly at his words. "From the church."

"Oh, thank goodness," she breathed. "I've been so worried. Since Joan passed, well... Arthur's not been himself. And now these people..." She gestured vaguely toward the waiting man. "They're not from round here - you can tell by how they move, like they're always ready to run."

"How long has this been going on?" Al asked gently.

"Started about a month after that article in the local paper," she replied. "You know, the one about the church's historical artefacts? Jan showed up at the Sunday service the very next week. Said she was a history student." The woman's face hardened. "My Thomas was a history professor at the university for thirty years. That woman doesn't know her Tudors from her teapots."

Standing on Arthur's doorstep, the door opened before Soapy's knuckles could touch it. Arthur stood in the doorway, his tall frame seeming to have shrunk overnight. Dark circles shadowed his eyes, and his usually neat cardigan was buttoned wrong. Behind him, the hallway which Joan had always kept bright with fresh flowers lay in shadow.

"Come in," he said, his voice carrying the weight of confession. "I need to tell you all something. I am afraid, I haven't been totally honest with you. First..." He gestured toward the sitting room. "Let me introduce Jan, an acquaintance of mine."

Jan stood by the cold fireplace, one hand gripping the mantel where Joan's photograph still watched over the room. Her carefully applied makeup couldn't hide the tension in her face, and her Manchester accent cut sharp against Arthur's gentle local tones as she offered a tight, "Hello."

Sam noticed how she positioned herself between Arthur and the door, like a wolf protecting its prey. The room felt cold despite the morning sun trying to pierce the heavy curtains.

"There's a fellow down the road," Sam said quietly, watching Jan's face. "Leather jacket, expensive watch, looking rather anxious. Would you like to explain who he is and why he's obviously waiting for you?"

The silence stretched taut as a wire between them. Jan's carefully manicured nails dug deeper into the wooden mantel, leaving tiny half-moons in the polish. Her eyes darted between Sam, Al, and Soapy, calculating odds like a cornered animal. Behind her, Joan's photograph seemed to watch the scene unfold.

"Well, well," she finally broke the silence, her Manchester accent thickening with each word. Arthur flinched at the harshness in her voice, so different from the gentle tones she'd used during their garden conversations. "Looks like you've caught us out, haven't you?" A brittle laugh escaped her. "That's my partner down there. Good little operation we've got going, we've found ourselves a nice little niche." Her lips twisted into something between a smile and a grimace. Vulnerable people in churches. They trust so easily, don't they, Arthur?"

Arthur made a small sound, like something breaking inside him. Al stepped closer to him, offering silent support.

"But you're just in time for the show," Jan continued, her voice taking on a manic edge. "Haven't quite sealed the deal with Arthur yet. Though we were close, weren't we, love?" She directed this at Arthur, who seemed to shrink further into himself.

"Your job is to prey on the grieving," Sam's voice cut through her performance like a blade. He shifted his position, placing himself more firmly between Jan and Arthur. The movement was subtle but deliberate - a shepherd protecting his flock.

Something in Jan's eyes turned feral. "Oh, look at you!" she spat, pushing away from the fireplace. Her heels struck Joan's carefully maintained hard wood floor like hammer blows. "The great detective, worked it all out, have you? Got it all figured?" Her voice rose hysterically. "What exactly do you think you can do about it? We'll just move on. We always do. There are plenty more churches, plenty more grieving widowers."

"To Manchester, perhaps?" Sam's quiet words landed like stones in still water. He watched her eyes widen and saw the slight tremor in her hands. "I imagine the police there would be very interested in your activities. Other widowers, other stolen artefacts..."

The change in Jan's expression was subtle but profound. The mask of defiance cracked, showing something underneath, not just anger now, but shame. Her eyes caught Joan's photograph and quickly skittered away as if the captured happiness there burned to look at.

"We haven't..." her voice faltered, then strengthened. "We haven't actually committed any crime here." But the edge was gone from her tone, replaced by something that might have been regret. Her shoulders slumped, and suddenly she looked tired, human. "I intended to, but..." She glanced at Arthur, and something raw flickered across her face. "Arthur's different. He reminds me of my dad, same way of puttering in the garden, same gentle way of offering tea even when his own heart's breaking..." She shook her head violently as if trying to dislodge unwanted memories. "I can't... I can't do this anymore. The whole thing's gone wrong." Her voice cracked on the last word. "We're leaving. You won't see us again." She moved toward the door, then paused, her hand on the handle. For a moment, she looked younger, uncertain. "I am sorry, Arthur," she whispered, then was gone, leaving only the echo of her footsteps and the lingering scent of her expensive perfume.

The front door clicked shut behind her, and Arthur's legs suddenly seemed to give way. He sank into Joan's favourite armchair, his face ashen.

"I've been such a fool," he whispered, his voice breaking. "Joan would be so ashamed of me."

"How do you feel?" Sam asked gently, kneeling beside Arthur's chair. The older man's hands trembled as he clasped them in his lap.

"I feel ashamed." Arthur's voice was barely audible. Then he looked up, meeting Sam's eyes for the first time. "But... relieved too. Like a weight's been lifted." He straightened slightly in the chair, some of his old dignity returning. "I couldn't do it; you see. Couldn't give them the bowl. Every time Jan asked about it, I'd hear Joan's voice..." He swallowed hard. "She used to polish it every Saturday, singing hymns under her breath. I just couldn't bring myself to give Joans bowl to Jan."

"Where is it now?" Sam asked softly.

"Hidden in the garden wall. Behind the loose brick where Joan used to leave messages for the grandchildren's treasure hunts." Tears welled in Arthur's eyes as he looked around at their faces. "Will everyone forgive me? The congregation, Peter... they all trusted me."

Sam placed a gentle hand on Arthur's shoulder. "You are forgiven," he said with quiet certainty. "Pastor Peter thinks the world of you. This won't change that - if anything, it will show them how even the strongest among us can need help sometimes."

Moments later, they were in the garden retrieving the bowl. Arthur's hands steady now as he reached into the hiding place. The bronze surface was dulled by earth but otherwise unmarked. Then as Al carefully wrapped it in his scarf, Arthur touched it one last time. "Joan used to say it looked most beautiful in the morning light," he murmured. "Like it was holding God's own sunshine."

Sam felt divine gratitude flood through him as they walked back to the Church. They had recovered more than just an artefact today. They had rescued a soul from darkness and guided a lost sheep back to the fold. Above them, though the morning was bright now, the North Star still faintly visible, a reminder that even in our darkest moments, God's light never truly leaves us...

CHAPTER 3

THE MEETING WITH PASTOR PETER

The bronze bowl had finally come home, catching the simmering colours of the sunset as it had for centuries. Pastor Peter stood before it, one hand hovering near but not quite touching, respecting the miracle of its return. Behind him, footsteps echoed on ancient stones as Sam, Al, and Soapy entered the church from the vicarage inner side doorway.

"Greetings, each of you," Peter turned, his eyes bright with unshed tears of relief. He cleared his throat. "I hope you are all well." His gaze kept returning to the bowl, as if afraid it might vanish again. "Thank you for bringing it back where it belongs. What a remarkable job you've all done!"

Sam stepped forward, placing a steadying hand on Peter's shoulder. "God's work, Peter. We were just His instruments."

"Yes, yes of course," Peter nodded, but his expression darkened like a cloud passing over the sun. "But now... now I'm worried about Arthur. How did he take it? Learning about Jan's true nature?"He began pacing the aisle, his footsteps echoing off stone walls that had witnessed centuries of prayers. "She's been manipulating him for weeks, hasn't she? Using his grief like... like a key to unlock his emotions."

"Like a wolf in sheep's clothing," Soapy murmured, his weathered hands clutching his hat.

"Exactly!" Peter's voice cracked slightly. "He must have thought she genuinely wanted friendship. After Joan... well, we all know how lonely he's been."

Sam watched the pastor's agitation with understanding.

"He had started to suspect," he offered gently. "We could see it in his eyes, the doubt he was feeling. He said part of him was relieved to have the truth finally exposed."

"Thank heavens you three arrived in time and unveiled her deception - well, your timing was truly amazing. Or should I say, God's timing?"

"Amen!" The word burst spontaneously from all three men, echoing through the empty church like a choir's response.

Peter stopped his pacing, turning to face them fully. His concern for Arthur lined his features.

"How was he after she left?"

Sam stepped into a shaft of coloured light from the windows, his face painted in fragments of blue and gold. "He was ashamed, at first," he said carefully. "But when we confronted Jan it was as if he was letting go of a burden he couldn't put down alone." He paused for a moment before asking, "What will happen now with Arthur? And what about Jan and her partner?"

Peter clasped his hands behind his back, his shadow long against the stone floor as he considered the questions. The silence filled only by the distant cooing of pigeons in the bell tower.

"Arthur comes first," he said finally, conviction growing with each word. "I'll go to him tomorrow, make it absolutely clear that he has nothing to fear from us. No judgment, no repercussions." He paused, swallowing hard. "I should have been there more, after Joan. Sometimes we all need..." His voice strengthened with resolve. "I think it's time I was more present for him. Sometimes we all need a helping hand, don't we?"

Silence fell again, but it was a thoughtful silence, filled with contemplation.

"And Jan?" Al's voice carried an edge now. "Her partner? We can't let them continue their predatory game. They need to be stopped before they target another grieving victim."

Sam caught Peter's eye, seeing the internal struggle there - the Christian call to forgiveness warring with pastoral responsibility.

"We have a duty," Peter said finally, straightening his shoulders. "To protect other congregations, other vulnerable people. I'll call the local clergy together, warn them about these... these wolves among the flock."

"The police should know too," Soapy suggested, his lined face creased with concern. "Inspector Matthews has always been good to us."

"Yes," Peter nodded, relief evident in his voice. "I will call them. We'll bring this dark chapter to a close properly, with both earthly and divine justice."

The rays of the evening light suddenly intensified, sending the bowl's reflection directly onto Joan's old pew where she used to sit every Sunday. They all saw it - a sign, perhaps, that their path forward was blessed.

"Joan would approve," Soapy said softly, and no one could disagree.

Sam turned to Pastor Peter and Soapy. His hand unconsciously touched the cross in his pocket, a gesture that had become familiar over the past two days.

"Pastor, Soapy," he began, his voice thick with emotion, "Al and I want to thank you for your hospitality. Being part of this, helping recover the bowl, supporting Arthur, it's shown us both what God can do when He brings the right people together at the right time." He glanced at Al, who gave a nod of agreement. "Would it be alright if we stayed one more night? Tomorrow morning we'll need to leave. There are other souls out there who might need help, other adventures God has planned."

Peter's face softened with genuine affection, the worry lines of recent days smoothing somewhat.

"Of course you can stay. How could we refuse two men who've brought such blessing to our congregation?" He shook his head in wonder. "You know, when Soapy first brought you here, I had no idea how much we needed you both. True men of God, you are. It humbles me to see how He works through you."

"Pastor," Sam replied, his voice catching slightly, "the blessing has been ours. Truly."

The evening sun caught the bronze bowl one last time, sending a warm glow across their faces. Peter glanced at his watch and straightened.

"I should get started on those calls - the other clergy need to be warned about Jan and her partner. And I must telephone Arthur..." He smiled warmly at them all. "I'll see you at breakfast. Have a blessed evening."

After Peter left, the trio made their way back into the vicarage. Soapy busied himself in the kitchen, his practical nature showing in how he prepared for their departure. His weathered hands carefully wrapped thick sandwiches in wax paper, tucking them into their small backpacks along with bottles of water and packets of biscuits.

"For the journey," he explained, his eyes suspiciously bright. "Never know when you'll need sustenance on God's path."

They shared a simple supper together, bread, cheese, and Soapy's homemade soup, talking quietly about their adventures and what might lie ahead. The North Star was already visible through the kitchen window, bright and unwavering, as they finally prepared for bed. That night, the old church seemed to wrap around them like a protective embrace, holding centuries of prayers and countless stories of God's grace.

GOD
will never
LET US DOWN

CHAPTER 4

BACK TO THE CANAL

A pale November dawn painted the vicarage windows in muted gold, frost crystallizing on the leaded glass. The North Star still gleamed faintly in the pewter sky. Sam found Al already at prayer, kneeling beside his bed, breath visible in the cold morning air. They packed their few belongings in silence, mindful of the sleeping household. In the church doorway, Sam paused, his hand resting on centuries-old oak now worn smooth by countless faithful hands.

"Thank you, Lord," he whispered, his words forming small clouds in the frozen air. "For bringing us here when we were needed."

The morning was bitter cold as they made their way toward the canal path, dead leaves crunching beneath their feet. Frost had transformed spider webs into delicate silver lattices between the bare hedge branches.

"You know, Al," Sam pulled his coat tighter against the chill, "before God found me, I was drowning in darkness. The drugs, the despair..." He looked up at the lightening sky, where the North Star was still visible. "But now His purpose is everywhere. That star isn't just a light - it's His hand guiding us forward."

Al stamped his feet against the cold, his face thoughtful. "I agree. That's no ordinary star Sam. It's God guiding us, showing us where he wants us to be.When I left the ministry, I thought I'd lost Him forever," he confessed, breath misting, "But walking this path with you..." He smiled, though his eyes glistened. "It's like the flames of love in my heart have been reignited. Thank you, Sam, for letting me share this journey."

Sam gripped his friend's shoulder. "Don't thank me. Thank God, He brought us together for His purpose, Al. Your pastoral heart, your experience - they're gifts we need on this journey."

The canal emerged through the morning mist, its dark waters reflecting the pale sky. A solitary swan glided past, leaving ripples in the stillness. Both men felt it - that sense of divine rightness, of coming full circle.

"Well, Al," Sam's voice was hushed with reverence, "we're back where it all began. This wonderful canal..."

"It feels like home," Al finished softly.

They hadn't gone far when a figure materialized from the mist ahead, a woman, her posture speaking of both urgency and fear. Her coat was buttoned wrong, as if dressed in haste.

"Greetings," Sam called out gently, noting how she was startled at their approach. "I'm Sam, and this is my friend Al. You look like you need some help?"

Relief transformed her worried face. "Oh, thank heavens! I'm Mary - Mary Goodbye. I've been searching for you since dawn." She glanced nervously over her shoulder. "Word spread about what you did at St. Michael's, how you helped Arthur." She stepped closer, lowering her voice. "I do need your help. My neighbour, Iris... something dark has taken hold of her. Something that shouldn't be."

Sam and Al exchanged knowing looks. The North Star might have faded, but its guidance remained clear.

"Perhaps we should talk somewhere private?" Sam suggested, seeing how Mary shivered - not just from the cold.

"We could go to my house," Mary suggested through chattering teeth.

Sam and Al followed Mary along the frost-rimed towpath, their footsteps crunching on dead leaves. The canal water looked black on the November morning, reflecting the leaden sky above. A bitter wind cut through their coats, carrying the metallic scent of approaching snow.

"It's not far," Mary said, hugging herself against the cold. "Just past the old lock keeper's cottage." She glanced nervously over her shoulder again. "I've been praying for help ever since... since the screaming started."

Sam and Al exchanged concerned looks.

"Screaming!" Al exclaimed, alarmed.

They turned off the towpath onto a narrow lane lined with Victorian workers' cottages. Bare branches reached for the sky like skeletal fingers, and somewhere a church bell tolled nine times, the sound hollow in the cold air.

"Iris and I used to walk to church together every Sunday," Mary continued, fumbling with her gate key. "She is my dearest friend. But since Thomas died..." Her voice caught. "Well, you'll soon understand."

Through a gap in the houses, Sam glimpsed at another cottage across the way, its windows dark despite the morning hour. Heavy curtains blocked any view inside, but even from the distance, something about the place made his skin crawl.

Inside Mary's warm kitchen, the kettle was soon whistling on the stove. Mary turned to them with desperate hope in her eyes. "Will you help? Can you save my friend's soul before it's too late?"

Sam touched the cross in his pocket, feeling that familiar divine guidance.

"That's why God led us here," he said softly. "Tell us everything."

Mary's hands cupped her teacup as if seeking warmth from the harsh morning's coldness. "You should have known Iris before," she said softly, her eyes fixed on a point across the room. "Every Sunday, rain or shine, we'd walk to church together. She had such a beautiful voice, used to lead the choir. Her faith was..." She paused, swallowing hard. "Well, it was an inspiration to us all."

Sam leaned forward in his chair, sensing there was more to come. "What changed?"

"It was after Thomas, her husband passed." Mary's voice saddened. "Cancer took him so quickly. One month he was tending his roses, the next..." She shook her head. "Iris stopped singing first. Then she stopped coming to Bible study. Said she couldn't bear to hear passages about God's plan when she couldn't understand why He'd taken Thomas."

"Grief can shake the strongest faith," Al murmured, his pastoral experience evident in his gentle tone.

"But it is more than that," Mary continued, setting her cup down with a slight tremor. "She started reading these books about communicating with the dead. Said if God wouldn't give her answers, she'd find them herself." Tears welled in her eyes. "I tried to warn her. Showed her Leviticus 19:31 - *'Do not turn to mediums or seek out spiritists, for you will be defiled by them.'* Then the board appeared."

"The board," questioned Sam. "Do you mean a Ouija Board?"

"Yes, yes," replied Mary, nodding, her tone rushed. "That's what they are called. Iris found it at an antique shop. She said it called to her. Within a week, she'd changed her name to Hecate. Started wearing all black, burning strange incense. The Iris I knew..." Her voice broke. "The Iris who used to bring soup to the sick and teach Sunday school - she just vanished."

"And now, are there others also involved!" Al asked grimly.

"Yes." Mary sighed dabbing her eyes with a handkerchief. "Iris says she's helping people find peace, find answers about their loved ones. But you should hear the sounds coming from her house during these sessions, the crying, the strange languages. Sometimes..." She lowered her voice. "Sometimes I hear Thomas's name being called, but it's not his voice. It's something else, something that makes my blood run cold. I saw that board in her front room, there it was, displayed right on top of her cabinet like some sort of... trophy. Hand-carved, she told me, specially made for 'communing with spirits.'" Mary's voice trembled on her last words.

Sam exchanged a concerned look with Al. "1 Samuel 28:7 warns us about the dangers of consulting spirits. It's like opening a door that was meant to stay closed. The people who mess around with these boards are utterly foolish. They have no idea!"

"It's not just foolishness," Mary's hands trembled as she set down her cup. "It's becoming something truly dark. When I tried to remind her of the verse of Deuteronomy 18:10-12, about not practising divination or consulting the dead..."

"Let no one be found among you who sacrifices their son or daughter in the fire,

who practices divination or sorcery, interprets omens, engages in witchcraft, or casts spells, or who is a medium or spiritist or who consults the dead," Al quoted softly.

Sam leaned forward, his face grave. "Jesus taught us to seek the living God, not commune with spirits. This is dangerous territory."

"I just want my friend back," Mary whispered. "The real Iris, not this... this Hecate she's become. Is there hope? Can you help her find her way back to God's light?" Mary's sad tone continued as she carried on with her story, the morning light casting long shadows across her sitting room.

"Last Tuesday's meeting was worst of all," she said softly. "I could hear them from my garden, chanting, crying out. Some sounded frightened, but Iris just kept pushing them to continue."

Al's face darkened with concern. "The name she is calling herself alone is a telling sign. Hecate was a goddess of witchcraft in ancient times. This isn't just playful experimentation anymore."

"No," Sam agreed, touching the cross in his pocket. "I Corinthians warns us clearly: *'I do not want you to be participants with demons. You cannot drink the cup of the Lord and the cup of demons too.*'" He leaned forward, his voice gentle but firm. "How many people attend these sessions now?"

"Twelve," Mary whispered. "Started with just three, but it's growing. Mostly vulnerable people, those who've lost loved ones, seeking comfort in all the wrong places." She twisted her handkerchief in her lap. "Last week, young Tommy Peters joined them. He lost his mother last month, poor boy. Only sixteen."

Sam and Al exchanged alarmed glances.

"The young are particularly vulnerable," Al said. "Their grief makes them perfect targets for dark influences."

"Iris wasn't always like this," Mary continued, rising to pace by the window. She looked out seeing the storm clouds were gathering, matching the heavy darkness of their discussion. "After her husband died, she started reading about spiritualism. Said the church's comfort wasn't enough, she needed to know, to be sure about the afterlife."

"The great deceiver often starts with our deepest wounds," Sam observed. "Takes our natural longing for comfort and twists it into something dangerous." He paused, listening for divine guidance. "When's the next meeting?"

"Tomorrow evening." Mary wrung her hands. "I've been praying for a way to stop it, but Iris won't listen to me anymore. Says I'm trying to keep her from her 'true calling.'"

"1 John tells us to 'test the spirits to see whether they are from God,'" Al quoted, his resolve evident in his tone. "Any spirit that draws people away from Christ's teachings is not of God."

Sam stood, moving to the window beside Mary. The canal was visible through the trees, its waters dark and choppy under the gathering storm.

"We'll need to approach this carefully," he said. "These aren't just lost souls we're dealing with - there's real spiritual danger here."

Thunder rumbled in the distance as if emphasizing his words. Mary crossed herself instinctively. "Will you help? Can you stop this before someone gets truly hurt?"

Sam turned from the window, his face set with purpose. "That's why God led us here, isn't it, Al? Right where we needed to be."

"Indeed," Al nodded gravely. "But we'll need to prepare ourselves spiritually. This isn't like recovering a stolen bowl. We're dealing with forces that actively oppose God's light."

"'*Put on the full armour of God,*'" Sam quoted, "'*so that you can take your stand against the devil's schemes.*'" He placed a comforting hand on Mary's shoulder. "We'll need to know everything you can tell us about these meetings, who attends, what happens. And most importantly, we'll need to pray. A lot."

Mary sighed deeply, the weight of her neighbour's situation clearly taking a toll on her. "It's such a shame," she continued, her voice filled with sorrow. "Iris has been a good Christian for the last four years, but ever since she got involved with that horrid spirit board, she has not been back to our church."

The kitchen grew darker as storm clouds gathered outside, but Sam's eyes were bright with divine purpose. He studied the cross hanging on Mary's wall, seeking confirmation of the plan forming in his mind. This was more than just a lost soul , this was spiritual warfare.

"Mary," he said quietly, his voice carrying that certainty that Al had come to recognize as God's guidance, "we can help bring Iris back. But we'll need to attend tomorrow's meeting, before the séance begins. Can you telephone Iris to arrange that?"

Hope bloomed on Mary's tired face. "Yes, yes of course!" She hurried to the hallway phone, her slippers pressing against the worn carpet. Through the wall, they could hear her voice, warm and casual, betraying nothing of her worry. When she returned, she was practically glowing.

"It's all arranged! Iris, I mean Hecate, no her name to me will always be Iris. Well, she said you're both welcome to observe. Even participate if you wish." She crossed her hands, relieved. "And please, stay here with me. I have a room with two single beds. Stay as long as you need."

The loud thunder rumbled outside as Sam nodded gratefully. "Thank you, Mary. We will also need something else - half a dozen blindfolds."

"Blindfolds?" Mary's eyebrows rose, but she didn't question it. "There are some in the church's junior cupboard. I can get them at tonight's prayer meeting."

While Mary busied herself clearing away the empty tea cups, Al leaned closer to Sam. His voice was low with concern. "Brother, we're dealing with serious deception here. That spirit board, it's gets its hooks in deep. This could take time." He glanced at the window, where rain had started to fall. "What exactly are you planning?"

Sam's eyes held that mysterious twinkle that always appeared when God was working through him. "Later," he whispered. "First, we pray. This is God's battle, not ours."

The storm grew stronger outside, but in Mary's kitchen, three souls bowed their heads in prayer, their faith a light against the gathering dark.

Later that evening, the church bell struck ten as Mary hurried back through the November darkness, clutching the blindfolds to her chest. Inside her warm kitchen, Sam and Al sat deep in prayer, their faces illuminated by candlelight.

"I've got them," she announced breathlessly, laying six black fabric strips on the table. "Sister Margaret uses them for the children's Easter play."

Sam picked one up, testing its opacity against the candlelight. "Perfect," he murmured. "God's plan is coming together." His fingers traced the cross in his pocket as thunder rumbled outside.

Al studied his friend's face. "You're sure about this?"

"The Holy Spirit's guidance is clear," Sam replied. "Tomorrow night, we'll see God's truth pierce through this deception."

The following evening, Sam and Al stood on Iris's doorstep. Red light spilled from her windows, and strange incense drifted on the bitter wind. The door opened to reveal a woman dressed in long flowing black robes, her face sharp with artificial mystery.

"Welcome," she smiled. "Please, come in and join our circle."

The parlour had become a temple to darkness. Black candles flickered in brass holders, their light catching the polished surface of the Ouija board centered on a round table. Strange symbols covered the walls where family photos once hung.

"Thank you, Hecate," Sam said carefully, using her chosen name. "Before we begin, would you accept a challenge?"

Hecate tilted her head, curiosity flickering across her face. "What sort of challenge?"

"Let everyone recite the Lord's Prayer while blindfolded. Then proceed with your séance as planned."

"But why?" For a moment, confusion cracked her mystical façade. "Why would we want to do that?"

Sam met Iris's gaze steadily, seeing past Hecate's carefully constructed facade to the wounded soul beneath. "I want to prove something to you," he said gently. "To show you the truth about these séances and free you from their hold." His voice carried the quiet authority of divine purpose. "With God's forgiveness and your Pastor's guidance, you can return to God's path. His grace is waiting for you, Iris." Sam watched her face carefully as he used her real name. Something flickered in her eyes - recognition, perhaps, or remembrance of who she'd once been.

The candlelight cast strange shadows as Iris considered his words. Outside, the November wind rattled bare branches against the windows like they were skeletal fingers tapping to seek entry. Finally, she spoke, her voice softer, more like her old self. "Your words touch my heart, young man. They remind me of... of better times." She swallowed hard. "Yes, I accept your challenge. Whatever way it goes."

The séance circle gathered; twelve souls seated around the ancient board. Black candles flickered in a sudden draft, though no window was open. Iris's hands trembled slightly as she addressed the group."Tonight is different," she announced. "Our guests, Sam and Al, have offered a challenge." Her voice caught slightly on the word 'challenge.' "We'll begin with the Lord's Prayer, then I want everyone to put on a blindfold before we start our... our work." She looked to Sam, something like hope fighting against fear in her expression. "Please, get ready to begin."

Sam and Al, their voices filled with conviction and faith, began to recite the Lord's Prayer. The words, so familiar and comforting, filled the room, each syllable imbued with a power that seemed to pierce the very darkness that had gathered there. *"Our Father, who art in heaven. Hallowed be thy name; Thy kingdom come; Thy will be done on earth as it is in heaven. Give us this day our daily bread. And forgive us our trespasses, As we forgive those who trespass against us. And lead us not into temptation; But deliver us from evil. Amen."*

As the final 'Amen' echoed, black fabric covered every pair of eyes. Darkness descended, broken only by the candles' glow. Fingers found the planchette, and Sam felt divine guidance strengthen in his heart. The moment of truth approached.

The candles dipped in the darkened room as Hecate's voice quavered in the silence. "Is there a spirit presence here? Please answer 'yes.'" The blindfolded participants waited, breath held, fingers light on the planchette. Nothing moved. Minutes stretched like hours. Sam could hear nervous shifting, the rustle of clothes, a caught breath. Still nothing. "Please," Hecate tried again, her voice less certain now, "name those present at this table." The planchette remained stubbornly still beneath their fingers. She cleared her throat. "Spirit, John celebrates his birthday tomorrow. Can you confirm this?"

The silence grew heavier. Where once the board had seemed to dance with supernatural energy, now it lay dead and powerless under their touch. Sam could feel Iris - not Hecate, but Iris - trembling beside him.

"Would... would anyone else like to ask a question?" The artificial mystery had fallen from her voice, leaving only uncertainty.

"Yes." Amelia's voice shook. "Spirit, please spell out your name. Make contact with us." Her plea hung in the air, unanswered.

The planchette remained motionless. No mysterious force guided their hands, no spectral presence made itself known. The power that had seemed so real, so seductive, had vanished like morning mist in sunlight. One by one, they removed their blindfolds. Candlelight revealed faces painted with confusion and dawning realization. The goddess Hecate, ruler of ghosts and darkness, had abandoned her namesake. Or perhaps, Sam thought, she had never truly been there at all.

"I don't understand," Iris whispered, her carefully constructed persona crumbling. "It always worked before. Always." The candlelight caught tears in Iris's eyes as she dismissed her followers. "It's over," she said simply, her voice stripped of its affected mystery. "The séance doesn't work. Please, everyone should go home."

The visitors filed out silently, confusion and disappointment heavy in their steps. As the door closed behind the last person, something remarkable happened. Like a mask falling away, Hecate's carefully constructed persona crumbled, leaving only Iris - the real Iris - standing in the parlour's dimming light. She turned to Sam and Al, tears streaming freely now. "Thank you," she whispered, her voice thick with emotion. "You truly are God's servants. During the Lord's Prayer..." She pressed a hand to her heart. "I felt His presence again, after so long." The words tumbled out faster now, as if a dam had broken. "I've been trapped in darkness for months, but now... Oh Lord, thank you!" She grabbed a tissue from a nearby box. "I'll call Pastor Mark first thing tomorrow. I need to come home to church."

Outside, the November night had grown bitter cold, but Sam and Al barely noticed as they walked back to Mary's house. Stars pierced the clearing clouds overhead, the North Star brightest among them.

"Well, Al," Sam's voice carried quiet wonder, "I knew God would work through us, but even I didn't expect such a complete transformation."

"The Holy Spirit moves in powerful ways," Al agreed. "To see her throw off darkness so completely..."

They spotted Mary at her door before she saw them, her silhouette anxious in the lamplight. Their smiles told her everything before they could speak.

"You two look like cats who've got the cream," she exclaimed, ushering them into her warm kitchen. "Did everything go well?"

Al couldn't contain his joy. "Mary, it was miraculous. Hecate vanished, and Iris returned to us. She's done with the séances, the Ouija board, all of it. Expect to see her in church soon."

"Once she stepped into God's light," Sam added, "the darkness lost all power over her. She won't lose her way again."

Mary beamed as she bustled about making tea. "Sit down, both of you. I've got something else I need your help with."

The kitchen clock ticked softly as Mary served tea and homemade scones, the warmth of their victory with Iris still lingering in the air. But something in Mary's expression suggested their work wasn't done.

"There's another matter," she began, setting down her cup with slightly trembling hands. "Something that's been troubling my spirit." The kitchen seemed to grow darker as she continued, despite the cheerful lamp light. "It's about a man called Joe Horton. He has this bible group."

Sam and Al exchanged glances, sensing divine purpose stirring again.

"He targets lonely women, particularly widows. to join his group" Mary's voice strengthened with certainty. "They all contribute to his cat charities that he runs, but when you telephone these places, it's always the same woman answering, backing up his stories." She leaned forward, lowering her voice further. "He seems perfect on the surface," Mary continued, her voice dropping. "Respected church member, runs charities for homeless cats, leads Bible study. But..." She twisted her handkerchief. "The ladies he targets all live alone, they have no-one to protect them. There is also a gentleman, Bob Styles, who he is friendly with. I'm concerned, maybe Horton is also setting him up to be a part of his group."

"Tell us more," Sam encouraged gently, touching the cross in his pocket.

The kitchen grew quieter as Mary outlined Joe Horton's web of deception. Sam leaned forward, his gift for discernment already active. "What happens when you try talking to the ladies in his Bible study?"

Mary's hands clenched around her teacup. "They're completely under his spell. He's got this way about him, charming, proper, everything a good Christian gentleman should be." Bitterness crept into her voice. "If he asks for money, they give without question. One lady even took out a loan last month for the 'new cat shelter.'"

"And Bob Styles?" Sam pressed. "Why would Joe want him in the group?"

"Bob's vulnerable, he lost his wife two years ago, inherited a nice sum." Mary's voice dropped. "Joe's been taking him to lunch, showing him these supposed shelters sites, he intends to use. Classic grooming, if you ask me."

Al, remembering his pastor experience, raised a gentle objection. "We need to be certain, Mary. False accusations against a brother in Christ..."

"I know Al, I've prayed about this for months," Mary responded firmly. "Asked God to show me if I was wrong. But every time I see Joe with those trusting women, every time I hear about another 'special collection' for the cats..." She shook her head. "The Holy Spirit keeps pressing on my heart that something's very wrong."

"How many women are in this group?" Al asked, his instincts alert by Mary's statement.

"Five. All regular donors." Mary's eyes filled with tears. "Our Pastor feels uneasy too. But Joe's so careful, so respected. He's a wolf in sheep's clothing. I have no doubts about that."

Sam studied Mary's face in the lamplight, noting the deep worry lines that appeared whenever Joe's name was mentioned. "This situation's is really troubling you, isn't it?"

Al leaned forward; his measured tone steady. "Let's examine what we know, Mary. Scripture warns us about false prophets who prey on the vulnerable for dishonest gain. But we need to be certain." He glanced at Sam. "There are two possibilities here - either Joe Horton is exactly what you fear, or he's a misunderstood brother in Christ doing legitimate work." The kitchen clock ticked heavily in the silence as Al continued. "I suggest we start with your Pastor. He knows Joe, knows the congregation. His insight will be valuable before we plan any action." He smiled gently at Mary. "What do you think?"

Relief flooded Mary's tired face. "Yes... yes, that's sensible. I'll go call Pastor Mark right now." She hurried to the hallway phone, leaving Sam and Al to exchange meaningful glances.

Mary returned to the kitchen, her mood lifted. "Pastor Mark will see us tomorrow morning at eleven," she announced, settling back into her chair. "He is concerned about Joe as well,- said he also has his doubts about him."

The kitchen had grown darker, the shadowy November night pressing against the windows. Suddenlt, the North Star shone steadily through a break in the clouds as if confirming their path forward.

"Perfect timing," Sam murmured, touching his cross. "God's hand at work again."

Together they sat in companionable silence, the kitchen clock marking time softly. Mary's cats curled up by the radiator, purring contentedly, such a stark contrast to the troubled thoughts of Joe's supposed cat charities that occupied their minds. The evening drew to a close with prayers and quiet determination. Tomorrow would bring new challenges, but for now, they had a divine purpose to guide them. As they prepared for bed, the wind picked up outside, rattling bare branches against the windows, the skeleton fingers tapping on the glass again.

"Sleep well," Mary called as they climbed the narrow stairs. "I know, God has led you here for a reason."

Sam and Al exchanged knowing looks. Just as with Iris, they would need all of God's guidance to expose whatever darkness Joe Horton was possibly hiding beneath a Christian facade.

GOD LOVES
YOU MORE
IN A MOMENT
than anyone could
IN A LIFETIME

CHAPTER 5

A PASTOR'S CONCERN

As they approached, the vicarage was surrounded by a misty dullness against the November sky, and frost crunched under their feet. Pastor Mark opened the door before they could knock as if he'd been watching for them. His weathered face bore the strain of sleepless nights.

"Welcome to my humble abode," he gestured them into the sitting room, where a coal fire fought against the morning chill. "Let's speak freely here."

Once they were settled, Mark leaned forward in his chair, hands clasped tightly. "Mary's spiritual discernment has never led us astray before," he began carefully. "And I must admit, Joe's behaviour with the ladies in his Bible group troubles me deeply. The way he operates..." He shook his head. "So polished, so careful. Too careful, perhaps."

The fire popped, sending shadows dancing across the walls as Mark continued. "He's clever, slippery as an eel when you try to pin him down about these cat charities. But Mary is closer to the situation than I am and sees things I can't. And what she's seeing..." He met Sam's eyes. "I don't like the sound of it," Pastor Mark continued, rising to stoke the fire. "Everything is so perfectly structured. The Bible study group meets in different homes each week - always the same pattern. He arrives early, charms his host, and by the time others arrive, they has already written a cheque for the latest 'urgent cat shelter need.'"

Mary nodded vigorously. "Last week it was Mrs. Henderson. She's still paying off the loan for her husband's funeral, but Joe convinced her the shelter needed new heating before winter."

"And Bob Styles?" Al asked, his instincts alert. "Mary mentioned he's being drawn in?"

Mark's face darkened. "Bob lost his wife Sarah two years ago. He is still raw with grief. It seems Joe has been cultivating him. Taking him to lunch, showing him supposed shelter sites. Always talking about how the ministry needs a man's perspective."

"The shelters," Sam interjected. "Has anyone actually visited them?"

"That's the clever part," Mary explained. "When you call, this same woman always answers. she says Joe's out inspecting other sites. Very convincing, very professional. But when I drove past the main shelter address..." She hesitated.

"It's an empty lot," Mark finished grimly. "Has been for years. But try telling that to his supporters. He's got an answer for everything, planning permissions pending, temporary setbacks. Always with that smile, that absolute certainty that God's blessing his work."

Sam leaned forward. "The woman who answers the phone - could she be part of it?"

"Must be," Mark nodded.

"The Bible study itself," Al asked. "What's the content like?"

Mary twisted her handkerchief. "Oh, he knows his scripture. Weaves it beautifully with stories about 'God's creatures needing our help.' Always ends with prayer, and usually a special offering for some urgent need."

"He's is definatly targeting the vulnerable," Mark said heavily. "Widows, lonely souls, those most desperate for purpose and connection. Using their faith against them." He ran a hand through his grey hair. "But proving it? Well, that's another matter entirely."

Sam felt the familiar touch of divine guidance. "The setup seems sophisticated," he observed. "Someone is obviously working with him - maybe several people. That could be his weakness."

"His Achilles heel," Mark agreed grimly. "If we can find the cracks in his facade..." his words drifted off.

Al turned to Sam, trust evident in his expression. "Where do we begin? Your gift for seeing God's path has never failed us. With Mary and Mark's help, we can end Joe's deception once and for all."

Sam touched the cross in his pocket, seeking divine guidance. "Joe's clever, too clever to confront directly. We need to be subtle." He began pacing before the fireplace. "First, we talk to the ladies in his group, but carefully. We can't let him become suspicious, do nothing to alert him." The morning light caught the frost on the window panes as Sam continued. "But the key might be a Trojan horse, someone who appears vulnerable, exactly the type Joe targets. She could gather information, discover his network." His eyes met Mark's. "And we shadow him, learn his routines, his contacts. Where he really goes when he claims to be at these phantom shelters."

Mark nodded slowly, understanding dawning.

"We'll need two people we can trust completely." Sam explained his plan. "One to play the vulnerable newcomer, another to follow Joe's movements." He looked to Mary. "Any thoughts on who might help?"

Mary nodded but she wanted to be sure. "I think we should leave things here for now to allow us time to go over all the aspects of our plan. These two individuals must be beyond reproach and fit for the purpose. They must have similar feelings towards Horton. I'm sure I will come up with at least two names of people who are able and willing to join us. Pastor, I will liaise with you because we know our church well enough to get the right individuals. So, is it okay if we reconvene this meeting at 7 pm?" Mary proposed.

Everyone agreed, and it was suggested that if they thought of any more ideas, they could use the afternoon to write them down.

That evening at 7 pm, everyone gathered at the vicarage to reconvene their meeting. They were all ready to continue with their discussion about what to do regarding Joe Horton.

Mary was eager to put her suggestions forward. "I've made a few choices. Firstly, there are the Davis mom and daughter, Chandice and Amy. Both ladies are solid and dependable. Chandice is talented and smart; Amy is very peaceful and positive. Chandice is about thirty, and her mom is about sixty. Both are good Christians. The next two are good friends in the church, and they also do projects together, like evangelizing. They are Alice and Ann, and they have been members for more than 25 years."

Evening shadows lengthened in the vicarage study as they weighed their options.

Pastor Mark also had a suggestion, "I suggest Ron and Ivy Jones they have both served faithfully in every church role imaginable. We should consider."

Sam touched his cross, feeling divine guidance settle his thoughts. "I think Chandice and Amy would be perfect. From what you have told me Amy seems to have the gentle spirit to play our Trojan horse, able to play the kind of vulnerable soul Joe targets. And Chandice..." He added slowly. "Her sharp mind and attention to detail make her ideal for surveillance."

The fire crackled as Mark considered this. "I think your right Sam, the Davis women are excellent choices. Their warmth disarms people and makes them open up. And their faith is unshakeable."

"Then we're agreed?" Sam looked around the room, meeting each person's eyes in turn. The divine purpose seemed to fill the space between them.

"I'll contact them tomorrow," Mark promised, his voice carrying quiet certainty. "With God's blessing, we'll meet soon and set things in motion."

"God's justice is coming for Joe Horton," Mary declared as they left the vicarage, her voice carrying quiet certainty on the November night. The North Star guided them home through streets silvered with frost.

Back at Mary's house, exhaustion from the day's planning settled over them. The magnitude of what lay ahead demanded rest, and they retired early, each lost in private prayer.

Morning brought renewed purpose with their breakfast tea. The kitchen clock had just struck ten when Pastor Mark's call came. Mary's face lit up as she listened.

"It's arranged!" she announced, returning to the kitchen. "Chandice and Amy will meet with us tonight at seven. Mark's set everything up." Her eyes sparkled with anticipation. "I took the liberty of accepting for all of us."

Sam felt that familiar divine guidance strengthen. "Perfect timing," he said softly. "God's hand is moving."

Al nodded, clasping his hands in gratitue. "Everything's falling into place exactly as it should."

The morning's light caught the frost still clinging to Mary's garden, making it sparkle like diamonds. Soon they would begin dismantling Joe's carefully constructed deception, bringing God's truth to light.

Sam, Al and Mary spent the afternoon in quiet prayer, seeking divine guidance for the task ahead.

The North Star was just becoming visible in the darkening sky when they arrived at Chandice and Amy's home, a welcoming cottage with warm light spilling from its windows.

Chandice greeted them at the door, her face bearing the serene strength that had made Mary think of her for this mission.

"Please, come in," she gestured them inside, where Pastor Mark was already seated with Amy in their cosy sitting room.

"I arrived early," Mark explained, "to prepare the ground." His eyes met Sam's, conveying silent confirmation that these were indeed the right allies for their cause.

Mary leaned forward, her voice low with urgency. "Joe Horton isn't what he seems," she began. "He's targeting vulnerable women through his Bible study group, all living alone, all trusting his supposedly charitable work with cat refuges." Her hands twisted in her lap. "He has professional leaflets and convinces them to set up monthly donations. But when you call these shelters, he's never there - just this mysterious woman who always answers."

Amy's gentle face hardened as she listened. "Using God's word to steal from widows," she said softly. "Like the Pharisees Jesus condemned."

"Exactly," Mark agreed grimly. "And we need your help to expose him."

The evening shadows deepened outside as Mark laid out the gravity of the situation. "These women's savings, their homes, everything they've worked for is at risk. Sam and Al have been led here by God to help us stop this."

Sam felt divine confirmation strengthen as he spoke. "My gift of discernment aligns with everything Mary and Mark have observed. This man must be stopped before more souls are harmed."

Silence fell as Chandice and Amy considered their words.

"He approached me about Mom joining his group," Chandice finally said, her accountant's mind analyzing the pattern. "Wouldn't take 'no' for an answer, but interestingly, never asked me to join. Always focused on Mom, living alone..."

Amy's gentle face showed steel beneath her warmth. "Like the serpent in Eden, using God's words for evil." She straightened in her chair. "I say we bring him down. The Lord doesn't look kindly on those who prey on widows."

"How can we help?" Chandice asked, her tone, serious.

The lamp light softened the determination on their faces as Mary outlined the plan.

"Amy, you'll be our Trojan horse. Join his Bible group, show interest but be hesitant about donations. We need to see how he operates from the inside."

Amy's gentle face showed steel beneath her smile. "I've dealt with plenty of scammers in my time. He won't see through me."

"Chandice," Mary continued, "we need you to track his movements. He walks to church, perfect cover for following him, seeing where he really goes."

"Consider it done," Chandice nodded, already planning routes and timings. "But what about this mystery woman who answers the phones? Could she be living with him?"

"That's what we need to find out," Sam said quietly. "Al and I will get closer to him at church and see what we can learn."

Pastor Mark surveyed the group, divine purpose evident on every face. "Then we're set. We'll meet up after afternoon service on Sunday evening, say seven o'clock at the vicarage. We can compare notes and plan our next move."

The North Star shone through the window as they rose to leave, its light steady and sure.

"God be with you all," Mark blessed them.

"Amen," they responded in unison, united in their mission to expose darkness to light.

THE WILL
of God prevails

CHAPTER 6

OPERATION - HORTON

Sunday morning light filtered through the stained glass, casting coloured shadows across the congregation. The covert team exchanged subtle glances, their plan already in motion. Amy spotted her opportunity when she saw Jess Hatt standing near Joe before the service. Moving with practised casualness, she approached them.

"Jess, dear! It's been too long." Her voice carried just the right mix of warmth and hesitation. "Are you in Joe's Bible group? I've been thinking of joining..."

Jess brightened immediately. "Oh, Amy, yes! You'd be so welcome."

Amy let satisfaction flicker briefly across her face. Phase one was working perfectly. Moving next to Joe, she watched his reaction carefully. "I've been talking with Jess about joining your group. She said I'd be more than welcome to join them"

Joe's smile was automatic, practiced, the kind that didn't quite reach his eyes. "We would love to have you." Instantly, he produced glossy leaflets from his jacket pocket with smooth efficiency. "Everything you need to know is here, times, locations..."

Amy accepted the papers, noting how professionally they were printed. Real money had gone into these. "Thank you, Joe. Looking forward to it." She made her way back to Chandice, making sure they didn't discuss anything that she had done, just in case someone was listening.

Sam felt divine guidance strengthen as he and Al approached Joe Horton. The cross in his pocket seemed to pulse with warmth, a warning, perhaps, of the spiritual battle ahead. Joe stood by the table under the archway. His movements were precise as he arranged his glossy leaflets, each gesture calculated to project trustworthiness.

"Hello, Joe." Sam let warmth fill his voice, though his heart beat faster with purpose. "I'm Sam. We've heard so much about your work here." Joe's handshake that followed was revealing, too smooth, too practiced, like a salesman's grip rather than a brother in Christ. "This is my friend, Al."

"Hello, Joe. Nice to meet you," Al added extending his hand out to Joe.

Joe's eyes moved over them with professional assessment, like a predator sizing up potential prey. Sam recognized the look from his street days, always searching for vulnerability, for opportunity.

Joe beamed a smile, "Welcome to our church family. Will you be staying long?" He inquired.

"We think so," Sam matched Joe's warmth while studying his reactions. "The outreach work here really speaks to us. And Pastor Mark, he's exactly the kind of spiritual leader we respect."

Something flickered behind Joe's carefully maintained facade at Mark's name, a tightening around the eyes, perhaps concern that the pastor might see through his performance. "Well, it's a pleasure to meet you both. I'm sure we'll see more of each other."

The morning light streamed through the stained glass, saints and martyrs watching in eternal vigilance, as Sam and Al took their seats. At the same time, Chandice maintained her surveillance during their fellowship with a watchful eye. Each conversation Joe initiated, every leaflet passed with practiced casualness, every 'chance' meeting with a vulnerable widow, all carefully noted for their evening meeting. Her mother's successful approach had already revealed Joe's eagerness to add another seemingly vulnerable soul to his flock.

Amy's whispered concern caught Chandice during the fellowship. "He's getting ready to leave. Are you prepared?"

"Don't worry Mum," Chandice's quiet confidence steadied them both. "I won't lose him." True to her word, when Joe slipped out of the church doors,

Chandice followed with practiced casualness. The November wind caught fallen leaves, swirling them around Joe's feet as he crossed the road toward town. His path led to Wilson Street, where he paused at number 19, the key in his hand glinting in the weak sunlight. Chandice waited in the shadows of a bare oak tree, counting seconds as Joe disappeared inside. Through the front window, she glimpsed an empty room, suspiciously empty, as if staged. After twenty minutes of silence, she retreated, the information secured.

The First Meeting

Later that evening the covert team gathered in the vicarage study, lamplight casting warm pools against darkened windows. The North Star shone steadily through breaks in gathering clouds as Pastor Mark welcomed them. "Make yourselves comfortable," he gestured to worn armchairs. "We have much to discuss."

Sam felt divine guidance strengthen as he began their report. "Al and I made first contact. He welcomed us exactly as expected. He played the role of devoted churchman without a flaw during service."

The vicarage study grew quieter then Amy shared her part. "I approached Jess first, she was eager to encourage me toward the Bible group." Her fingers smoothed her skirt as she continued. "Then I spoke with Joe directly. Very polite, very prepared." She handed over two glossy leaflets. "His complete setup, right here." The leaflets passed from hand to hand in the lamplight, each person studying them intently. Professional printing, careful wording, everything designed to project legitimacy.

"The information is all there," remarked Al. "The Bible group meets at Horton's house every Tuesday. If Amy goes to the next meeting, she can see if there is anything untoward when she attends," he suggested.

Everyone went silent for a while.

"Well, guys, let's hear what Candice has to say after tailing him," added Sam. "Chandice?" Sam prompted gently. "What did you learn?"

Chandice sighed, her frustration evident. "I got his address, 19 Wilson Street. Watched through the front window, but the room was empty. Almost too empty. Waited twenty minutes, saw nothing else." Her sharp mind was troubled by the missing pieces. "Not much, but it's a start."

"Indeed it is," Mark's pastoral voice carried quiet approval. "We've made first contact, gathered initial intelligence. Consider this our foundation day. God's timing is perfect, let's build on this and continue another watch on tuesday when he has his bible study meeting."

"I've got a car, so being near our master scammer's residence isn't a problem." Added Mary. She turned to Sam, "Would you and Al join me in my car? So, if there is any tailing to be done, you and Al will be there, which gives you an eye witness account of what happens. I will feel safer with you two supporting me in this surveillance operation."

"Sure," replied Sam. "Sounds good to me."

"And I'll make sure to get Mom safely inside," Chandice confirmed, "then take up my post."

The fire crackled softly as they finalized their plans. Pastor Mark cleared his throat. "One thing I should mention, I won't be able to join you Tuesday evening. There's a pastoral emergency in the neighbouring parish. The minister there is ill, and I've been asked to help."

"We'll manage," Sam assured him, touching his cross. "God's guidance is clear."

The North Star shone steadily through the study window as Mark blessed their mission. "May God's truth be revealed on Tuesday. Have a blessed, fruitful evening."

Tuesday Evening

The November evening wrapped Wilson Street in the early darkness. Two cars maintained their vigil, Chandice's closer to number 19, Mary, Sam and Al sat stationed in Mary's car further down the road, all watching Joe Horton's house with quiet intensity.

Inside, Amy found herself in a front room transformed from its earlier emptiness. Comfortable chairs had appeared, arranged in a circle, with Bibles and notepads laid out with careful precision. The empty stage was now set for its performance.

Joe began with practiced sincerity, his voice carrying the smooth authority that had convinced so many. "2 Corinthians 9:6," he intoned, "'*Remember this: Whoever sows sparingly will also reap sparingly, and whoever sows generously will also reap generously.*'"

Amy watched him move around the circle, noting how his eyes lingered on each member's face, assessing their receptiveness. His voice grew softer, more intimate as he continued, "And verse 7: '*Each man should give what he has decided in his heart to give, not reluctantly or under compulsion, for God loves a cheerful giver.*'" These verses speak directly to our calling," Joe remarked, gesturing to carefully arranged leaflets about his cat refuges. "Giving is paramount, not just in spirit, but in practical support of charitable causes. I take the charities I support very seriously indeed, as you may well know, particularly those who have been with my generous group for some time. Now everyone follow the Bible verses with pen and notebook at the ready."

Jess Hatt suddenly commented, "Most of us are givers to your charities, dear Joe. So, why ask for more donations from us?"

Joe smiled his usual convincing smile. "Yes, Jess, one can always find a little extra to give, but I'm thinking more of newcomers like Amy. We are so blessed to have her in our group tonight."

"Thank you," muttered Amy. "I am by nature a cheerful giver, so I'm clearly moved by what you have said, dear Joe. Please understand, I will show favour soon to the charities you mention. They are good and wholesome and very dear to me," she continued. This statement stuck in Amy's craw. While she was making it, Amy thought, 'I have said these things to help bring down this scammer character. Lord, please forgive me.'

Each member of the group was then asked to read one of their favourite New Testament verses. When they hhad finished, Horton told them how he had enjoyed listening to their readings, and with that, he brought the class to a close with prayer. Once the bible study was over, Amy realises that she was the only newcomer, said her goodbye's and left, making her way to Chandice's car. And since there were no new folk at the bible class, there was no one to tail, so they drove home.

The 2nd conflab meeting at the Vicarage

The following evening, the vicarage study held a tense atmosphere as they gathered for their second meeting. Lamplight caught worried faces as Mark began the debriefing. "Let's begin," he said softly, but concern shadowed his eyes. "Chandice? What did you observe?"

She shifted in her chair, the precision in her movements at odds with her evident frustration. "Dropped Mom off, maintained position, but" Her fingers drummed restlessly on her knee. "No new visitors, no suspicious departures. Nothing really to report."

Mary reached over and squeezed Chandice's hand. "You did exactly right. Sometimes what we don't see tells us as much as what we do."

"Amy?" Mark prompted gently. "The meeting itself?"

Amy's face tightened as she recalled the evening. The fire popped, sending sparks up the chimney as she gathered her thoughts. "He's masterful at manipulation," she began, her voice carrying quiet anger. "Started with Corinthians, perfect verses about generous giving. You could feel him weaving scripture into his web."

Sam leaned forward, his cross warm against his chest. "Which verses exactly?"

"2 Corinthians 9:6 and 7," Amy recited. "'*Whoever sows sparingly will also reap sparingly.*'" Her voice took on a bitter edge. "He wielded those words like weapons." Pausing, she took a deep breath. "When Jess questioned the constant requests for donations," she continued, hands clasped tightly in her lap, "he turned it so smoothly. Made it about newcomers like me, while making the regular contributors feel special for their 'faithfulness.'" She shook her head. "Every single member gives to at least one of his charities. I played along, hinted I'd join them soon. The smile he gave me..." She shuddered slightly.

"Nothing from our position," Mary added, but her eyes were on Sam, who sat silent, his gaze distant.

The North Star blazed suddenly brighter through the window as if it was highlighting his deep contemplation.

"Sam?" Al prompted softly. "You're seeing something."

"God's showing me patterns," Sam said finally, his voice carrying that quiet certainty they'd come to recognize as divine inspiration. "Joe's methods, his careful scripture selection, the empty front room that transforms for meetings..." He stood, moving to the window where the star shone. "It's all theatrical, carefully staged performances to manipulate faith into funds."

"But how do we prove it?" Chandice asked, her practical nature seeking concrete evidence.

Sam turned from the window, purpose lighting his face. "God's revealing a new direction. "I sense we need a change," Sam said finally. "God's showing me a new direction." He touched his cross, feeling its warmth. "We need to extend our plan."

The fire crackled, sending shadows dancing across faces filled with renewed purpose. Something in Sam's tone suggested their real work was just beginning. The weight of his conviction pressed down on the room like a tangible force. His eyes, typically calm and measured, now burned with a spiritual fervour that both intimidated and inspired those around him.

"We only seem to be making minor progress," Sam began, his voice a low, gravelly whisper that carried the weight of deep spiritual insight. "Not enough to ensnare this super scammer. We need a breakthrough." A momentary pause hung in the air, thick with anticipation. "The spirit of truth has conveyed to me," he continued, his voice taking on an almost prophetic tone, "that Jess Hatt is another instrument in our divine plan, a potential ally willing to work with our team and help bring down this trickster."

The room seemed to hold its collective breath. Sam's gaze swept across the faces of his companions, each person absorbing the spiritual implications of his words. "I propose Amy contacts Jess," he declared, his certainty resonating with an almost tangible energy. "I am convinced she knows more about our trickster than we do and has valuable information to share."

Amy shifted in her seat, a complex mixture of determination and uncertainty playing across her features. When she spoke, her voice was steady but soft, carrying an undercurrent of resolve. "Of course, it's alright," she responded, her eyes meeting Sam's with a blend of trust and trepidation. "We must bring down the scammer. Let's get it done." A ghost of a smile flickered across her lips.

Pastor Mark, seated in his favourite worn armchair that seemed to echo the wisdom of countless counselling sessions, nodded slowly. His presence was a calming balm, a spiritual anchor amidst the group's mounting tension.

"Yes, this could be done," he mused, his voice carrying both gentleness and strategic precision. "I'll phone Jess and see if she is available to speak with Amy about the Bible group. I could just say she isn't totally happy with Horton. See what reply she comes back with. I'll play it by ear."

Approval rippled through the group like a silent wave, each member's subtle nod or shifted posture proving they were unified together in their support.

The Phone Call

Pastor Mark steadily dialled Jess's number. The ring tone hummed through the receiver - once, twice - then clicked into Jess's crisp

"Hello?"

"Jess, it's Pastor Mark." He kept his voice warm but weighted with purpose.

"How can I help, Pastor?" Something in Jess's tone suggested she'd been waiting for this call, though she might not have known it.

Mark's free hand found his Bible, drawing strength from its familiar leather. "What I'm about to share isn't easy, Jess, but it's necessary." He paused, seeking divine guidance for his next words. "There's a group of us, Mary, Chandice, Amy, Sam, and Al. God's brought us together for a purpose. We've discovered Joe Horton isn't what he seems. He's..." The words caught briefly in his throat. "He's using scripture to deceive, a wolf among our flock."

The silence that followed felt charged with spiritual energy. Through it, Mark could almost sense Jess's mind working, pieces falling into place.

"I've been waiting," she said finally, her voice carrying both relief and conviction. "Ever since Sam and Al arrived, I knew God was moving. I've had... doubts about Joe. The constant demands for money, the way he twists scripture..." She drew a sharp breath. "Yes, Pastor. I want to help. God's hand is clearly in this."

Mark felt divine confirmation surge through him.

"Thank you, Jess. We're meeting tomorrow night at seven, here at the vicarage."

Her warm chuckle carried through the line. "Most of them already know me, Pastor. But Sam and Al will need proper introductions."

As Mark set down the phone, the North Star seemed to pulse brighter. Another piece of God's plan had fallen into place.

Meeting at the Vicarage introducing Jess Hatt

The November rain tapped against diamond-paned windows, while inside, ancient radiators hissed and clicked, fighting the evening chill.

Pastor Mark knelt from his leather armchair, his prayer rising like incense in the hushed room. The others formed a circle around him, Mary perched on the edge of a worn wingback, Chandice and Amy sharing the old leather sofa, Al standing by the bookcase, his hand resting on a well-worn Bible. Sam had taken a position by the window, where the North Star pierced gathering storm clouds like divine reassurance.

As the final "Amen" faded, Mark's hands remained clasped, knuckles white with emotion. The door opened with deliberate quiet, and Jess Hatt entered their sacred circle. She moved with the controlled grace of someone used to staying unnoticed, her conservative dress and sensible shoes a perfect camouflage for her sharp intelligence. Her eyes, deep brown and watchful, assessed each person in turn.

"Sister Jess," Mary breathed, half-rising in welcome. They'd sung in the choir together for years, never guessing they shared the same suspicions.

"Mary." Jess's smile was warm but brief. She settled into the offered chair, adjusting her position until she could see every face clearly. "Thank you all for trusting me with this."

Chandice leaned forward, her accountant's mind already working. "I hear you've been gathering evidence?"

"For months." Jess's fingers found her wedding band, twisting it as she spoke, a habit formed in the seven years since John's passing. "I positioned myself exactly where God wanted me, another widow in his Bible study, another potential donor to his fictional charities."

Al pushed away from the bookcase, concern etching his features. "It must have been difficult, maintaining that pretense."

"Not as difficult as watching him twist scripture into chains," Jess replied, righteous anger flashing across her face. "But it paid off. I found his weakness,

Trixie Dodd, 29 Grove Place."

Sam turned from the window so quickly the floorboards creaked. "Near Hampstead Heath?" His voice carried the tension of divine revelation.

"Minutes from Wilson Street," Jess confirmed, triumph replacing anger. "She's the one who always answers his charity phone line. But she's more than that. I've seen them together when they thought no one was watching, sharing private jokes, speaking in whispers."

"The missing piece," Amy whispered, exchanging meaningful looks with her daughter Chandice.

"God's timing is perfect," Pastor Mark said softly, rising from his chair. "He led us to each other, piece by piece. Sam and Al helping Mary with Iris, Mary's suspicions about Joe, Chandice and Amy's surveillance, and now..." He gestured to Jess. "The key to it all."

The fire had burned low, casting amber shadows across intent faces as Sam crossed the room and sat down. Wind rattled the study windows, but inside, holy purpose warmed the air. "We need to confront Trixie directly," Sam said, touching his cross for guidance. "Al and I will visit her unannounced. She won't have time to prepare her defences or warn Joe. One conversation might unravel their entire deception."

Pastor Mark's weathered face showed careful consideration. His fingers stroked his chin. "There's wisdom in that approach," he said slowly, measuring each word. "Trixie might be waiting for an opportunity to unburden her conscience. Sometimes people trapped in deception are looking for a way out."

Around the room, faces showed varying degrees of hope and determination. Chandice sat straight-backed, her mind already cataloguing potential evidence. Amy's gentle features had hardened with resolve. Jess's eyes gleamed with the satisfaction of knowing the exposure of Joe Horton was near.

"Once we have proof," Sam continued, divine certainty strengthening his voice, "we take everything to the police. This isn't just about money anymore, it's about protecting God's people from those who would exploit their faith."

Mary, who had been watching the interplay of shadows on the study walls, spoke with quiet force. "I agree with Sam," she said, her soft voice carrying unexpected authority. "Confront Trixie directly. The simplest path is God's path."

Pastor Mark rose, signalling the meeting's end. "Then we're agreed. Sam and Al will visit Trixie." He looked around the circle of faces, each one called by God for this purpose. "Let's close in prayer."

As they bowed their heads, the storm outside grew stronger, but they were sheltered by divine purpose. The trickster's reign was ending, and they would be instruments of God's justice.

The November morning wrapped Grove Place in crystalline frost, each breath visible in the bitter air like ascending prayers as Sam and Al approached number 29, their footsteps crunching on frozen grass.

Trixie stood in her perfectly maintained garden, expensive leather gloves failing to warm trembling fingers. Dried leaves crumbled in her grasp as she registered their presence. Her carefully constructed image, the designer jacket, the salon-perfect hair seemed suddenly like armour about to fail.

"Trixie." Sam infused his voice with gentle authority, watching her shoulders tense. "How are you this morning?"

"I'm fine." The words came too quickly, too brightly. Her eyes darted between Sam and Al, professional charm warring with rising panic. "Can I help you with something?"

Al maintained a strategic distance, reading the fear beneath Trixi's polished surface. The cross in Sam's pocket warmed as he spoke their carefully chosen words.

"We're from the Church near Wilson Street. We need to discuss Joe Horton."

The name struck like lightning. Something fundamental cracked in Trixie's carefully maintained facade, not just her composure, but the walls she'd built around her guilty conscience. Dead leaves scattered down from lifeless fingers, dancing away in bitter wind like abandoned lies.

Her immaculate living room spoke of desperate control, everything arranged with mathematical precision, expensive art positioned to impress. But as Trixie sank onto her pristine white sofa, that control finally shattered.

"I can't..." her voice broke. "I can't do this anymore." Tears threatened her perfect makeup. "He's planning worse things now. A dating agency scam targeting lonely hearts. Romance fraud." Raw pain filled her words. "I've watched him manipulate those women in his Bible study, using their faith. And I..." Mascara traced black rivers down her cheeks. "I'm so sorry but I love him. But he doesn't care. It's all about the money for him. He knows I'm in love with him and he's just.... just," her voice quivered. "Taken advanatge of my feelings for him."

Sam and Al exchanged knowing looks as divine confirmation strengthened their purpose. "Then this is is your moment of redemption," Sam said softly. "Let truth break these chains. This hold he has over you."

Something shifted in Trixie's tear-stained face, defiance replacing years of submission. "He thinks I'm just his blonde puppet?" Steel entered her voice. "Well, this puppet's been keeping records. Every transaction, every scheme, every penny stolen from trusting souls." She straightened, throwing off invisible shackles. "I'll give you everything. Bank records, fake charity documents, all of it. I'll testify. This ends today." She stood up, moving swiftly over to the bookcase. Removing several books from the top shelf, she pulled out a brown folder. "Here you are," she said handing Sam the folder, her tone determined to finish the hold Joe had over her. "This has every record I kept."

Sam's final words were a blend of encouragement and strategic guidance. "You are blessed, and you will get full support and help, everything you need. But for now it's important that you don't tell him anything. Don't arouse his suspicions."

The morning sun broke through gathering clouds, flooding the room with golden light, heaven's approval of truth finally spoken, of one soul stepping from darkness into light.

The next morning, Mary's sitting room transformed into an impromptu war room, November sunlight filtering through her lace curtains to illuminate the evidence of Joe's deception. Sam and Al hunched over Mary's dining table, their shoulders nearly touching as they pieced together Joe's web of lies. Hundreds of bank statements, donation records, and Trixie's careful logs. Page after page, all amounting to years of calculated fraud. Even, the air seemed charged with purpose, heavy with the scent of Mary's brewing tea and decades of polish on dark wooden furniture.

"You'll need something to keep you going," Mary said softly, appearing with a plate of her famous egg and cress sandwiches. You've been at this for hours."

Al stretched his ink-stained fingers, accepting a sandwich gratefully. "Mary, this is extraordinary," he said, gesturing at Trixie's records. "Look at the detail here, all documented with perfect precision."

Sam lifted another stack of papers, his weathered face tightening. "She tracked everything," he said softly. "Every widow's 'donation', every manipulated bank record." He touched his cross, thanking God for revealing the maze of deception. "She wasn't just an accomplice, she was gathering evidence all along."

Mary settled into her armchair, its worn velvet catching the strengthening sunlight. "Perhaps God was working through her guilt," she suggested, "turning her shame into purpose."

"This changes everything," Sam said finally, divine certainty strengthening his voice. He spread several key documents across the polished table surface. "Every scheme, every victim, every penny he has taken under false pretences - it's all here."

"Then I think I should ring everyone and set up our next meeting." Mary said, standing she walked into the hallway to the telephone table. Her fingers trembled slightly on the rotary dial as she began making calls, the old phone's ring echoing through the quiet room. "Tonight," she announced between calls, triumph colouring her voice. "Seven o'clock at the vicarage. Yes, yes, everyone's coming."

Moments later, Mary returned back into the sitting room. Her eyes sparkled with satisfaction. "Well done, guys," she congratulated Sam and Al. "Just wait until they all see this. Everything is arrange. We meet tonight at the vicarage at 7 pm tonight."

Meeting at The Vicarage - Summary of evidence

The vicarage study pulsed with a palpable energy, a mixture of anticipation, moral clarity, and hard-won vindication. Soft evening light filtered through stained-glass windows, casting ethereal shadows across the faces of those who had fought a silent war against deception.

Pastor Mark's introduction was a masterpiece of measured emotion. His hands, clasped together with a blend of gentleness and strategic intent, spoke volumes before he uttered a word. "Hi, everyone," he began, his voice carrying the weight of their collective journey. "Thank you for attending this significant meeting."

Sam stepped forward. His eyes, sharp, intelligent, swept across the room. Each colleague recognized the profound transformation their investigation had undergone. "Without going into too much detail," Sam began, his voice steady and deliberate, "we established ourselves with Trixie. She was a woman trapped in a web of manipulation; her love weaponized against her."

The room held its collective breath.

Sam's narrative unfolded like a carefully constructed argument. Horton's method was laid bare, a calculated exploitation of devotion, using Trixie as a shield for his fraudulent operations. Financial records, charity scam details, systematic deception, each document was a wound inflicted on their community's trust.

Al sat beside Sam, his presence a silent corroboration. Their partnership, built on trust, and moral conviction was evident. They were more than just mere investigators; they were true men of God.

Mary's eyes glistened with a complex mixture of emotions, relief, vindication, a deep-seated anger at the violation of trust. Her first voiced concerns about Joe Horton had been crucial.

Pastor Mark's response was controlled yet profound. His connections in law enforcement would be the final instrument of justice. "I'll will contact the police and hand this folder over to them. We will meet here on Sunday evening before evening prayers,"his voice carrying the weight of institutional authority.

The meeting concluded not with celebration, but with a solemn understanding. They had done more than expose a fraud. They had restored the sanctity of their community's trust.

By Saturday morning, Chief Inspector John Gordon had transformed their meticulously gathered evidence into legal action. Horton was arrested and placed in custody; his network of deceit finally unravelled.

The Last Gathering.

The November sunset painted the vicarage study in amber and gold, while the North Star shone through stained glass with particular brilliance, as they gathered one final time. Each person sat where divine purpose had placed them. Mary near the fireplace, its warmth matching her practical faith; Chandice straight-backed in her chair, still processing figures in her mind; Amy and Jess sat together on the comfortable couch, Sam and Al flanking the window like protectors of scared text.

Pastor Mark stood before his ancient desk, its surface scarred by generations of pastoral work. His hands, steady now with justice accomplished, rested on a leather Bible passed down through decades of ministry.

"My dear friends," he began, voice rich with emotion. "Chief Inspector Gordon's call came this morning." He looked at each face in turn - faces that had become family through their sacred mission. The lamplight caught tears in his eyes. "Joe Horton has made a full confession."

Mary reached instinctively for Amy's hand, while Chandice's shoulders relaxed for the first time in weeks. Jess's eyes gleamed with the satisfaction of a hunter whose prey had finally been caught. Sam felt his cross pulse warm against his fingers, divine confirmation of their path.

"He's admitted to previous frauds as well," Mark continued, moving to pour communion wine into delicate glasses. "Trying to reduce his sentence through cooperation. But Trixie..." His expression softened with pastoral compassion. "Her meticulous records, her position as both accomplice and victim, the Inspector believes she'll receive suspended sentence. A chance for true redemption."

"God's mercy manifests in unexpected ways," Sam observed softly, his compassion showing in every word. "Even through pain, He makes a path to healing."

Mark lifted his glass, the wine catching evening light like liquid rubies. "To God's perfect justice, and to each of you, His chosen instruments of truth."

The room's atmosphere transformed like dawn breaking after longest night. Mary wiped joyful tears as she embraced Amy and Chandice. Sam and Al exchanged knowing looks filled with divine purpose fulfilled. Jess beamed a smile of pure gratitute.

"The North Star guided us true," Sam said quietly, watching darkness gather outside. Yet heaven's light still shone steady through the window, promising new adventures ahead. His cross felt warm - a reminder that their work for God never truly ended.

"Will you stay?" Mary asked suddenly, looking at Sam and Al. "Our church needs men like you."

Sam smiled gently. "Thank you Mary. Al and I will be happy to stay with you for a few more days, and then we must continue on Gods path following the North Star. But for now," he paused sensing God instructing him. "For now, I do believe our work here is not yet over."

CHAPTER 7

CONFRONTING THE SOOTHSAYER

The first light of dawn crept through Mary's guest room windows, casting a soft golden glow across the modest furnishings. Sam stirred first, his hands reaching instinctively for the well-worn Bible that had been his companion through his journey. The room seemed to breathe with the quiet anticipation of another day of purpose.

"It's time to hit the sack," he had murmured the night before, his voice carrying the gentle weariness of their recent victory against Horton. Now, in the early morning stillness, Sam and Al began their morning ritual of prayer and meditation, a practice as essential to them as breathing.

Al's reflection broke the morning silence.

"I like the work we do," he said, his voice filled with a mixture of gratitude and resolve. "God helps us resolve all challenges we have come against."

Sam nodded, understanding the deeper meaning behind Al's words. Their mission was more than mere investigation - it was a spiritual calling, a path of service guided by something greater than themselves.

"This is part of our destiny, Al," he responded. "We are helping folk who are in need. Getting the right results is very gratifying."

The room seemed to vibrate with their shared conviction, a manifestation of their faith and purpose.

Over breakfast, Mary sat contemplating whether to reveal the troubling thoughts she had been having over the last few weeks. She had meant to mention them to Sam and Al before now, but they had all been so busy, first helping Iris and then trying to expose Joe Horton that she felt God would guide her when the moment was right. After breakfast prayers, the warmth of her kitchen was a sharp contrast to the spiritual chill in her heart and she knew it was now the right time to tell Sam and Al about Duncan.

"He's... different from Joe Horton," Mary said, twisting her handkerchief. "Not after money, at least not directly. He speaks of aliens, of cosmic revelations." Her eyes sought Sam's, worry evident. "My friend Lucy says he's gathering followers. Claims he can channel extraterrestrial wisdom."

Sam felt his cross grow warm, a warning of spiritual deception ahead. Al's pastoral years showed in his furrowed brow. They had seen such false prophets before, wrapping lies in mystical language to ensnare searching souls.

"He calls himself a 'cosmic messenger,'" Mary continued, rising to pace before her fireplace. "Lucy says some of her church members are already under his influence. Speaking of star people, of secret knowledge..." Her voice trembled. "She's frightened for them."

"God's truth is stronger than any deception," Sam said quietly, divine purpose strengthening his words. "We'll help Lucy confront this darkness. Can you arrange for Al and I to meet your friend Lucy?"

"Of course," Mary replied. She hurried out into the hallway, reaching the telephone table, its aged wood warm in the lamplight. Her conversation with Lucy was brief but purposeful. When she returned, hope had replaced worry in her eyes.

"Six o'clock tonight," she announced. "Lucy's so relieved you'll help. She lives in the cottage on Church Lane."

Outside the morning's grey clouds suddenly cleared, and a winter sun bathed the kitchen in a golden hue. Sam smiled at Al, sensing this was heaven's confirmation of their next mission. The two friends exchanged knowing looks. Another wolf had entered the fold, but God's light would expose his darkness.

Lucy Fairchild's cottage stood like a guardian at the edge of Church Lane, its Tudor beams dark against whitewashed walls. Winter roses still bloomed in her garden, defiant against the November frost, while the North Star shone steadily above the ancient thatch.

"Lucy," Mary called softly as they approached. "These are my dear friends I told you about. This is Sam and this is Al." She introduced.

Lucy beamed at them, her hazel eyes crinkling at the corners. She appeared to be in her early 30s, with a kind face and auburn hair pulled back in a tidy bun. She wore a simple but elegant cream sweater and a long brown skirt.

"Welcome Sam and Al! Please, do come in," she said, ushering them into her cozy living room decorated with warm colours, and plush furniture. Oak beams crossed a low ceiling, while an inglenook fireplace dominated one wall. Family Bibles and devotional books lined shelves between leaded windows. "Please, make yourselves comfortable."

Sam felt divine guidance strengthen as they settled into chairs arranged around the hearth. His cross in his pocket which his mother had given him before she died pulsed warmly in his fingers, a confirmation to him that they were where God needed them.

"Lucy's been a rock in her church for years," Mary explained, accepting a cup of tea. "But this situation with Duncan..."

Lucy's hands trembled slightly as she set down the teapot. "He's clever," she said quietly. "Started with UFO talk, harmless enough, or so it seemed. But then..." She twisted her silver cross necklace. "He began claiming other things."

Sam nodded understandingly. "We're happy to listen and help in any way we can, Lucy. Why don't you tell us more about what's been going on?"

Al leaned forward, reading deeper worry in Lucy's eyes.

Lucy took a deep breath. "Well, Duncan started coming to our church a few months ago. At first, he was just very interested in UFOs and such. But then..." She paused, her brow furrowing. "He started claiming he was a clairvoyant and psychic. He began approaching vulnerable members, especially the elderly, and making these vague predictions."

"What kind of predictions?" Al asked, his eyes narrowed.

"Oh, you know," Lucy waved a hand, "saying he could sense a promotion coming their way, or that he detected a curse from a past life that he could remove, for a price, of course." She shook her head in disgust. "He even started asking for personal possessions, credit card numbers, social security information... said he needed it for special rituals. It's just not right."

Sam and Al exchanged a knowing glance. They had seen this kind of manipulation before. "You're right to be concerned, Lucy," Sam said, placing a comforting hand on her arm. "These frauds always prey on people's fears and insecurities. It's despicable."

Lucy's shoulders sagged with relief at his validation. "I'm so glad you understand. I've shared my worries with my own pastor, James. He's a wise and godly man. I know he doesn't approve of Duncan's actions either."

"It's good that Pastor James is aware," Al said. "Perhaps we could speak with him as well, get his take on the situation."

"Oh certainly!" Lucy replied eagerly. "In fact, I told Pastor James I was meeting you both and he said he's heard many good things about you two from Mary's pastor, Mark. About how you helped expose that conman Joe Horton schemes."

Sam shifted humbly in his seat. "We were just doing what we felt called to do. I always strive to listen to God's leading, to let Him guide my steps."

"That's one thing I respect so much about you, Sam," Al said proudly. "You have a real gift of discernment. I know if you sense something isn't right with this Duncan character, then it must be true."

Sam smiled gratefully at his friend before turning back to Lucy. "I do have an idea about how we might expose Duncan's deception..."

Lucy leaned in intently.

"Please, do share! I'm open to anything that would shed light on the truth."

As Sam explained his plan for himself and Al to attend church that Sunday and carefully approach Duncan afterwards to discern his true nature and intentions, Lucy found herself nodding along, a newfound sense of hope kindling in her chest. She had a feeling Sam was just the man to navigate this challenging situation with wisdom, boldness, and grace.

After further discussion and a heartfelt prayer together led by Sam, the group rose to say their goodbyes. Lucy embraced first Sam, then Al.

"I can't thank you enough," she said, her voice thick with emotion. "You've brought me such peace of mind already. I look forward to seeing you both at church this Sunday! I'll be sure to introduce you to Pastor James and of course to Duncan after the service."

"We'll be there," Sam promised. "You can count on us."

Mary stepped forward and squeezed Lucy's hands. "I'm so glad this meeting was helpful, my friend. I'll be praying for you all at my Church on Sunday. Sam and Al are staying over at mine at the moment, so they can tell me how things go when they get back from meeting this Duncan fellow."

With that, Sam, Al and Mary left Lucy, their hearts filled with shared purpose, faith, and solidarity for the trial ahead. As Mary drove off into the deepening dusk, Sam and Al sat in her car silently contemplating the role they were to play, guided by the still, small voice of the Almighty.

The congregation at the church erupted into enthusiastic applause as Pastor James concluded the service with a heartfelt prayer. The atmosphere was warm and inviting as people began to make their way towards the minor hall for tea and biscuits. Sam, and Al navigated through the crowd, their eyes scanning the room for Lucy and the mysterious Duncan.

As they entered the minor hall, Lucy spotted them and waved them over. She then discreetly pointed out Duncan, a heavy-set man standing at about 5 feet 10 inches tall, engaged in conversation with a small group of people.

Sam and Al exchanged a glance, silently communicating their shared determination to uncover the truth about this man. Approaching Duncan, he looked up at them with a curious expression.

"Hello, is it Duncan?" Sam asked politely. "I'm told you're the guy who knows about UFOs. May I introduce myself? I'm known as Sam, and this is Al, my buddy."

Duncan's eyes lit up with interest. "Yes, that's me. Nice to meet you both. What do you want to know?"

Sam smiled disarmingly. "I just have an interest. Where do you think these UFOs come from?"

Duncan didn't hesitate. "Well," he said confidently, "my view is UFOs come from outside the Earth, therefore extraterrestrial. What do you think?"

Sam tilted his head thoughtfully. "My first thoughts, UFOs come from this realm."

Duncan shook his head, a slight smirk playing at the corners of his mouth. "I have to disagree. I have seen many UFOs over the last few years. I can tell you categorically, UFOs are extraterrestrial. No doubt at all."

"Well, Duncan, I've never seen a flying saucer, so obviously you have the advantage," Sam conceded graciously. Then, shifting the conversation expertly, he asked, "Do you have any other interests?"

Duncan's eyes gleamed with a mix of pride and cunning. "Ah! Yes, I do. I'm a gifted clairvoyant and psychic."

Al leaned forward, feigning intrigue. "That's very interesting. Sam and I have always thought how good clairvoyants and psychics could be, so helpful to people in need."

Duncan pounced on the opportunity.

"Would you like to have a private consultation or come to one of my meetings? There will be a few people there. Many of them are from the Church."

Al glanced at Sam, "Okay, we will like to come to one of your meetings," he responded. "I'm sure it wll be intresting."

Duncan paused for a moment, mentally shuffling his schedule.

"Ah, I still have room in my Monday evening meeting, 7 pm, sharp. I like people to be punctual, so no waiting for folk to arrive. Get straight on with it. My address is 16 Bell Lane, round the corner from the church. See you both then."

With that, Duncan excused himself and melted back into the crowd. Sam and Al made their way back to Lucy, who was waiting for them with an expectant look on her face.

"Hi, you two. How did you get on with that crafty blighter?" she asked, her voice low.

Sam smiled triumphantly. "We have both been invited to a group meeting tomorrow evening, 7 pm sharp at his house, so the first part of the mission is complete."

Lucy nodded, relief and determination mingling in her expression. "Very good. Great result, guys. Right, it's time I was heading home. We can have a conflab after your meeting with the crafty blighter."

Wishing Lucy a pleasant day, Sam and Al made their way to Mary's house, where she greeted them warmly.

"Hi, guys. How did things go?" Mary asked, ushering them inside.

Sam settled into a comfortable armchair.

"Pretty good for a first introduction. We have arranged to meet with him tomorrow at his house at 7 pm. This soothsayer likes people to be punctual, he was very adamant about that."

Mary nodded, a pensive look on her face. "That's a good result so far. Great descriptive name for him, soothsayer. What's he like to deal with?"

Al leaned forward, his elbows resting on his knees.

"Very on the ball, business-like, can be a bit abrupt, forceful at times, likes folk to be obedient to him. We'll find out more when Sam and I attend his meeting tomorrow evening."

Sam's expression hardened with resolve. "Great assessment of the soothsayer. He is all those things. We can add to the list: devious and charlatan, with money on his mind, relieving people of their hard-earned cash. He's a dangerous fella, very clever, sharp, and to the point always, as Al said, business-like on everything that can harm him in any way, shape, or form." He paused, his eyes burning with a fierce determination. "He's a professional, it's going to take time to expose him. He's a smart, crafty blighter, but he will make mistakes. That's when we must be ready to counter-attack. We won't get this guy easy but get the soothsayer we will."

Al nodded in agreement; their faces set with the same unwavering commitment to the cause. But even in the midst of the uncertainty, there was a shared sense of purpose, a deep conviction that they were doing the right thing. They knew that the road to exposing Duncan's deception would be long and difficult, but they also knew that they had the truth on their side. And so, with hearts full of faith and minds sharpened with strategic intent, Sam and Al began to plan their next moves, confident that, in the end, justice would prevail.

Sam and Al arrived at Duncan's residence at 16 Bell Lane promptly at 7 pm the following evening, just as instructed. They were greeted by the self-proclaimed clairvoyant and psychic, who ushered them into a dimly lit room where a small group of people had already gathered.

Within moments, Duncan stood before the group, his demeanour exuding confidence and authority.

"Welcome one and all," he began, his voice smooth and persuasive. "Nice to see everyone here on time, so let's get started. I'm a clairvoyant and psychic all rolled into one. These are my gifts." He paused, letting his words sink in before continuing. "Each one of you will be entitled to a one-to-one session for a modest sum of £40 for each person, £50 for couples. Nice saving there, only a modest amount. It's a giveaway for what you'll receive in return from me."

Sam and Al exchanged a subtle glance, both noting the manipulative nature of Duncan's pitch. They watched as the others in the room leaned forward, their eyes wide with a mix of hope and desperation.

"So, what's in it for you?" Duncan asked rhetorically. "Plenty of good things can happen. Those of you suffering from stress and anxiety will find some relief. Money worries could cease. Good fortune awaits those who trust in me." He began to pace the room, making eye contact with each person as he spoke. "For the modest sum I have mentioned, my one-to-one consultations will reveal to me your needs and how best I can help you. I have good mentoring qualities which are invaluable in today's fast-paced, pressured world. My gifts will set you right. Some may even win money."

Sam fought the urge to shake his head in disgust. The way Duncan preyed on people's vulnerabilities was sickening. But he maintained a neutral expression, not wanting to blow their cover.

Duncan's voice took on a more commanding tone.

"You must always take my advice. I'm the one who has these incredible gifts. Your future depends on what I see through my psychic powers. I will guide you around any problem areas. My rituals are for your benefit." He paused, a sly smile playing at the corners of his mouth. "There will be other charges, modest sums of money. It's all about trust. I'm the dominant factor. My psychic power allows me to see your future, also your family's future."

Duncan clapped his hands together, making several people jump.

"So, who's signing up for one-to-one? Very important. C'mon! C'mon! Don't miss out. It's all yours."

To Sam and Al's dismay, nearly everyone in the room rushed forward, eagerly pressing money into Duncan's outstretched hands.

"Ah! That's more like it. Great, everyone," he said, his voice dripping with satisfaction. "I'll text you the date and time of your session."

As the group dispersed, Sam and Al hung back, pretending to fumble with their wallets. They handed over the money, forcing smiles as Duncan gripped their hands a little too tightly in a handshake.

Once outside, Sam let out a heavy sigh. "That was intense," he muttered, shoving his hands in his pockets.

Al nodded, his brow furrowed.

"The way he manipulates people... it's hard to watch. But at least we're one step closer to exposing him for the fraud he is."

Making their way back to Mary's house, they were both lost in thought. Mary greeted them at the door, her face etched with concern. "How did it go?" she asked, ushering them inside.

Sam collapsed onto the couch, running a hand over his face.

"It was... eye-opening," he said. "Duncan definitely has a way with words. He knows exactly what to say to get people to part with their money."

Al sat down beside him, nodding in agreement.

"He's got the whole 'trust me, I have special powers' act down pat. It's no wonder so many fall for it."

Mary listened intently as they recounted the evening's events.

"It sounds like he's even more cunning than we realized," she said, shaking her head. "But we can't let him continue to take advantage of people like this."

Sam sat up straighter, a determined glint in his eye. "Absolutely not," he agreed. "We need to come up with a plan to expose him, to show everyone the truth about who he really is."

The three of them stayed up late into the night, discussing strategies and possibilities. They knew it wouldn't be easy, but they also knew they couldn't stand by and do nothing.

As the clock ticked towards midnight, Mary stifled a yawn.

"We should probably get some rest," she said, standing up and stretching. "We'll need clear heads if we're going to outwit Duncan."

Sam and Al murmured their agreement, and soon the house was quiet, each of them retreating to their rooms to sleep. But even as they drifted off, their minds were still whirring, piecing together the puzzle of how to bring Duncan's deception to light.

The morning after their initial meeting with Duncan, Sam and Al found themselves eagerly anticipating the next step in their mission. As they sat at Mary's kitchen table, sipping coffee and enjoying a delightful breakfast spread, Sam couldn't help but check his phone every few minutes.

"Waiting for a message from our friend Duncan?" Al asked, a knowing smirk on his face.

Sam chuckled, setting his phone down. "I guess I'm just anxious to get started. The sooner we can expose him for the fraud he is, the better."

Mary, who had been bustling about the kitchen, paused to place a comforting hand on Sam's shoulder.

"I know you boys are eager, but remember, patience is a virtue. The Lord's timing is always perfect."

Sam smiled up at her, his eyes filled with gratitude. "You're right, Mary. Thank you for the reminder."

Just then, Sam's phone buzzed, causing all three of them to jump. Sam snatched it up, reading the message aloud:

"Session time 6:30 pm, tonight."

Al let out a low whistle. "Well, looks like we've got our marching orders. Better make sure we're on time, we don't want to give Duncan any reason to be suspicious."

Sam nodded, his face set with determination.

"Agreed. But first, I think we should spend some time in prayer and meditation. We need to make sure our hearts and minds are in the right place."

Mary beamed at them, her eyes shining with pride. "That's a wonderful idea, boys. You know where to find the quiet spot in the living room. Take all the time you need."

And so, Sam and Al settled into the cozy corner of Mary's living room, their Bibles open on their laps. For the next few hours, they lost themselves in the pages, each seeking out the perfect verses to guide them through the challenges ahead.

As the afternoon sun broke through the morning clouds, Al stretched, closing his Bible with a contented sigh.

"I don't know about you, but I could use some fresh air. What do you say we take a walk in the park?"

Sam agreed, and after telling Mary of their plans, the two set off. As Sam and Al stepped out into the November afternoon, they were greeted by a crisp, cool breeze that hinted at the approaching winter. The sun, though still bright, hung lower in the sky, its rays casting a golden glow across the landscape. The air held a unique blend of dampness and crispness, a signature of the transitional season. Fallen leaves, now drained of their vibrant autumn hues, crunched beneath their feet as they walked, a reminder of the cycle of life and the inevitability of change. The scent of a promised snowfall lingered in the air, a promise of the frosty days to come. It was the perfect weather for a reflective stroll, a chance to clear their minds and steel their resolve before their crucial meeting with Duncan.

As they strolled along the winding paths, the cheerful chirping of parakeets caught their attention. Sam paused, watching as a particularly colourful bird flitted from branch to branch.

"You know, there's a story behind these little guys," Al said, coming to stand beside him.

Sam turned to him; curiosity piqued. "Oh? Do tell."

Al grinned, always happy to share his knowledge.

"Well, legend has it that about 20 years ago, there was an accident involving a transport of exotic birds, right in the heart of London. The crates broke open, and all the parakeets escaped, making Hyde Park their new home."

Sam's eyes widened, impressed. "Wow, that's incredible. And now they've spread all over, huh?"

Al nodded; pride evident in his voice. "Yep. You can find them in parks all across the country now, Walsall, Sandwell, West Bromwich, you name it. They've really made themselves at home."

The two continued their walk, marvelling at the resilience of the parakeets and the beauty of the park. They stopped to admire a particularly stunning sparkling iced-over pond, the delicate silvery veins of crystalised ice shimmering in the late afternoon sun.

"You know, Al," Sam said softly, "moments like these... they really put things in perspective. The world can be such a harsh, unforgiving place at times, but then you see something like this..." He gestured to the pond, a smile playing at the corners of his mouth.

Al placed a hand on his friend's shoulder, understanding in his eyes. "It's a reminder that there's still so much good in the world, isn't it? That beauty and hope can be found, even in the darkest of times."

Sam nodded; his heart full of peace. "Exactly. And it's up to us to protect that good, to stand up for what's right, no matter how difficult it may be."

With a renewed sense of purpose, the two made their way back to Mary's, ready to face whatever challenges the evening might bring. As they entered the house, Mary greeted them with a warm smile.

"Welcome back, boys! How was your walk in the park?"

Al grinned, his eyes sparkling with joy. "Oh Mary, it was just what we needed. The trees, the birds... it was like a little slice of heaven."

Mary chuckled, gesturing towards the dining table. "Well, I'm glad to hear it. Now, I've prepared a special meal for you two, a hearty chicken broth to give you strength for your meeting with Duncan."

Sam inhaled deeply, the aroma making his mouth water. "Mary, you're an absolute angel. Thank you so much."

As they sat down to eat, Sam couldn't help but feel a sense of gratitude wash over him. Here he was, surrounded by the love and support of his dearest friends, about to embark on a mission that could change many lives for the better.

"Mary, this broth is incredible," Al said between spoonsful. "You've really outdone yourself."

Mary waved off the compliment, but her smile was one of pure delight.

"Oh, hush. It's the least I could do for my two favourite boys."

When the meal drew to a close, Sam and Al insisted on taking care of the dishes. They worked side by side, laughing and joking as they scrubbed and dried, their bond stronger than ever.

Finally, the time had come to prepare for their meeting with Duncan. They retreated to their rooms, each choosing their attire with care. They wanted to appear approachable but also convey a sense of professionalism and authority.

An hour later they reconvened in the living room, Mary stood waiting, her hands clasped in front of her.

"Now, you two listen to me," she said, her voice filled with a mixture of concern and pride. "I know you're doing the Lord's work, but please, be careful. Duncan's a tricky one, and I couldn't bear it if anything happened to you."

Sam stepped forward, enveloping Mary in a tight hug. "We'll be careful, Mary. I promise. And we'll be back before you know it, victorious and ready to celebrate."

Al joined in the embrace; his voice thick with emotion. "Thank you, Mary. For everything. We couldn't do this without you."

With final words of encouragement and love, Sam and Al set off into the evening, their hearts full and their minds focused on the task at hand. The November chill hung in the air, the crisp breeze a stark reminder of the impending confrontation. They paused for a moment to offer up a silent prayer before they knocked on the door, ready to face whatever lay ahead, secure in the knowledge that they walked with God and that the truth would always prevail.

Duncan opened the door, his smile a little too wide, his eyes a little too bright. He ushered them inside, into a small, dimly lit room with just three chairs, one for each of them.

Sam frowned, his eyes adjusting to the gloom. "Why the dim lights?" he asked, suspicion lacing his voice.

Duncan's grin widened, his teeth glinting in the low light. "Ah," he said, his voice dripping with false sincerity, "this is a sacred room, and lights have to be dim so I can focus better on your futures with my sixth sense." He gestured for them to sit, then he sat down and leaned forward. "Guys, I see both of you with issues. My perceptions are forecasting imminent danger on two fronts. Firstly, your finances are somewhat depleted. Your monthly incomes fall below your outgoings, so very soon, you will both hit the buffers."

Sam and Al exchanged a glance, their expressions carefully neutral. They knew this was coming, the classic setup for a scam. But they remained silent, allowing Duncan to continue.

"Secondly, your spiritual needs are great. Fortunately, you have come to me at the right time. I, and I alone, can save you from these oncoming disasters. Be sure these severe threats are very real. Both of you don't have any control over the unseen disasters that are about to hit you, but I do."

Duncan's voice had taken on a fervent, almost manic quality. His eyes gleamed with a predatory light as he leaned even closer.

"I can make your lives much better than they are right now. It's all about trust. Both of you should have confidence in me and my psychic powers. I can steer you clear of all adversities."

Sam fought the urge to recoil, to put distance between himself and this man who radiated deceit. But he maintained his composure, nodding slowly as if considering Duncan's words.

"It's clearly up to you," Duncan continued his tone coaxing. "What do you want to happen in your futures? Carry on the same, or change for the better? When you change, it's ongoing, always put your trust in me. You will both see good results in your lives. Things will become positive instead of negative. Your finances will improve. Money worries will no longer haunt you. Your relief is imminent. No more sleepless nights." He paused, his gaze boring into each of them in turn. "All I need is your trust in me. As for your spiritual needs, the same thing: confidence in what I say I can do and your total belief that I will deliver what I say. Your commitment to me must be total, without fault. No blameworthiness."

Duncan sat back, his expression one of false concern. "In short, guys, do you trust me to deal with your financial matters and your spiritual well-being? I guess I'm asking for you to give a limited power of attorney, as far as your finances are concerned. Listen, fellas, I need you to trust in me. I've done my best to explain what I see through my gifts. All I need to add is if you trust in me, you'll never regret it. My powers will astound you."

Sam hesitated, glancing at Al. They had known this moment would come, the point where they would have to feign agreement to gain Duncan's trust. But the reality of it, the oily persuasiveness of Duncan's words, made his skin crawl.

"Yes, I agree with all you have said here, Duncan, about trusting in you," Sam said slowly, choosing his words with care. "Of course, I have total trust in you handling some of my finances, and your psychic powers sound remarkable. You are a gifted person. But is it possible to allow Al and I time to take it all in? Your fascinating offer is, without doubt, worth supporting. It would be foolish to miss out."

Duncan's eyes narrowed, a flash of irritation crossing his face. "While I hear what you and Al are saying, for me, I would very much prefer a 'yes' from both of you this evening if you have complete trust in me and my clairvoyance skills. This, guys, is where I'm at," he retorted, his tone hardening.

Sam's mind raced. He knew they had to tread carefully, to find a way to appease Duncan without fully committing. He could feel the weight of Al's gaze on him, the unspoken question hanging in the air.

"Duncan, can we have a provisional consensus between the three of us, and you can advise us in some ways?" Sam suggested, his heart pounding in his chest.

To his relief, Duncan's expression softened. "Ah, okay, guys, we have a deal. Let me tell you what this means financially. Be prepared to hand over more cash, £100 at our next session next week."

Sam nodded, pretending to be confused. "Sure. What do you need the additional cash for?" he asked innocently.

Duncan waved a hand dismissively. "Good question. Let me first answer this way. First, my expenses, dealing with your spiritual needs to ensure your well-being needs are met by my fees. All your benefits will become apparent in the next few weeks." He stood abruptly, ushering them towards the door. "So, guys, let's leave the answers there for now. I've one more appointment tonight. I'll be in touch soon. Have a pleasant journey home."

Sam and Al allowed themselves to be shepherded out, their minds reeling.

"Thank you, Duncan. Al and I have enjoyed this new way that will bring us a better understanding of our lives and hopefully a more prosperous future," Sam managed, the words tasting like ash in his mouth.

Duncan grinned, his teeth flashing in the dim light of the hallway.

"Fab, guys. You'll be hearing from me," he said, before closing the door firmly behind them.

As they made their way back to Mary's house, Sam turned to Al, his expression troubled.

"Wow, that was so intimidating, Al. What was your impression of our first session?" he asked, his voice low.

Al shook his head, his brow furrowed.

"Well, Sam, same as you. He's a well-rehearsed guy and, as you said, intimidating, practically suffocating," he responded, his tone grim.

They walked in silence for a moment, each lost in their own thoughts. The crisp November air swirled around them; the scent of impending snow sharp in their nostrils.

Finally, Sam spoke, his voice filled with determination.

"We have to be careful, Al. Duncan's clever, and he's not going to be easy to expose. But we can't let him continue to prey on the vulnerable. We have to find a way to stop him, no matter what it takes."

Al nodded, his expression mirroring Sam's resolve.

"Agreed. We'll need to be smart, to play along until we have the evidence we need. But we will bring him down, Sam. I know we will."

With that, they continued on their way, their steps heavy with the weight of their mission. The road ahead would be difficult, fraught with danger and deceit. But they knew they had each other, and more importantly, they had the truth on their side. And with that knowledge, they could face whatever challenges lay ahead with courage and faith.

Mary paced the living room, her heart racing with anxiety as she waited for Sam and Al to return from their meeting with Duncan. The clock ticked loudly in the silence, each second stretching into an eternity. When she finally heard the sound of the front door opening, she rushed to greet them, her face etched with concern.

"Sam, Al! Thank goodness you're back," she exclaimed, pulling them both into a fierce hug. "I've been so worried. How did it go? Are you alright?"

Sam returned the hug, drawing strength from Mary's warmth.

"It was intense, Mary," he admitted, his voice strained. "Duncan's a force to be reckoned with. He had us on the back foot from the moment we walked in."

Al nodded, his face pale.

"I've never felt so intimidated," he confessed, sinking into a nearby chair. "The way he talked, the way he looked at us... it was like he could see right through us like he knew exactly what buttons to push."

Mary's heart ached for her friends. She could see the toll the evening had taken on them, the shadows of doubt and fear in their eyes. She sat down beside Sam, taking his hand in hers.

"I can't even imagine how difficult that must have been for you both," she said softly, her voice filled with empathy. "But you stood your ground, didn't you? You didn't let him break you."

Sam managed a weak smile.

"We tried, Mary. But it cost us. Literally. We had to agree to pay him another £100 next week. He's got us on the hook now."

Mary's eyes widened in shock.

"That's outrageous!" she cried, anger flaring in her chest. "The nerve of that man, extorting money from innocent people like that!"

Al sighed heavily, his shoulders slumping.

"That's not even the worst of it. The way he manipulates people; the way he preys on their fears and vulnerabilities... it's sickening. We've got to find a way to stop him, Mary. We can't let him keep doing this."

Mary nodded; her jaw set with determination.

"You're right, Al. We can't let him get away with this. But we need to be smart about it. We can't rush in blindly."

Sam leaned forward, his elbows resting on his knees.

"I know, Mary. But after tonight, I'm more convinced than ever that we're doing the right thing. Duncan's not just a fraud; he's a danger to everyone he comes in contact with."

Mary's expression softened, her eyes filling with compassion.

"I'm so proud of you both," she said, her voice thick with emotion. "I know how much courage it takes to stand up to someone like Duncan. But you're not alone in this. I'm here for you, every step of the way."

Sam and Al looked at her, their faces filled with gratitude.

"Thank you, Mary," Sam said, his voice barely above a whisper. "We couldn't do this without you."

Al nodded in agreement.

"Your faith in us, your strength... it means everything to us."

Mary smiled, tears glistening in her eyes. "That's what family is for," she said simply. "We lean on each other, we support each other, no matter what."

They sat in silence for a moment, each drawing comfort from the other's presence. Finally, Sam stood up, her expression resolute."I think it's time we brought this to the Lord," he said, his voice filled with conviction. "We need His guidance now more than ever."

Mary and Al nodded, rising to join him. They clasped hands, their heads bowed in reverence as Sam began to pray.

"Heavenly Father," he said, his voice ringing with faith, "we come to you tonight with heavy hearts, burdened by the weight of the task before us. We know that the path ahead is fraught with danger and deception, that the enemy seeks to lead your children astray."

Mary and Al murmured their agreement, their grip on each other's hands tightening.

"But we also know that You are with us, Lord," Sam continued, his voice growing stronger. "That You will never leave us or forsake us, that Your love and Your truth will guide us through even the darkest of times."

Tears streamed down their faces as they poured out their hearts to God, seeking His wisdom and His strength. As they prayed, a sense of peace settled over them, the fear and doubt melting away in the face of His unwavering presence.

When they finished, they looked at each other, their faces glowing with renewed hope and determination.

"We can do this," Sam said, his voice filled with quiet conviction. "With God on our side, we can face anything."

Al nodded a fierce light in his eyes. "Duncan may think he's untouchable, but he's about to learn the power of faith in action."

Mary smiled, her heart swelling with love and pride, as she listened.

"You two are truly doing God's work," she said softly. "And I know that, no matter what happens, He will see us through."

With that, they retired to their rooms, their minds and hearts at peace. The road ahead would be long and difficult, but they knew they walked it together, united in their love for each other and their unshakable faith in the Lord. And with that knowledge, they could face whatever challenges lay ahead with courage and grace.

The next morning, Sam, Al and Mary gathered around the kitchen table, their faces etched with determination as they discussed their plan to gather more information about Duncan's manipulative practices. The morning sun streamed through the windows, casting a warm glow over the room, but the atmosphere was charged with a sense of urgency and purpose.

Sam leaned forward, his elbows resting on the table as he spoke.

"I think our first step should be to reach out to some of the people who have attended Duncan's sessions," he said, his voice filled with conviction. "We need to understand what they've experienced, what they've been asked to agree to, and if they've felt any pressure or intimidation."

Al nodded, his expression grave. "Absolutely, Sam. And we should also try to find people who have been part of his group for a while. If we can talk to someone who's been under his influence for an extended period, they might be able to give us valuable insights into how he operates."

Mary listened intently, her brow furrowed in thought.

"You know," she said slowly, "I might know where to start. Lucy mentioned a couple to me a while back - Don and Marion Berry. They've been attending her church for years, and I think they might have had some dealings with Duncan."

Sam's eyes widened, a spark of hope igniting in his chest.

"That's great, Mary! Do you think you could reach out to them? See if they'd be willing to talk to us?"

"Of course, Sam." Mary replied, smiling in agreement. "I'll give them a call right now. If they're open to meeting with us, it could be a real breakthrough."

As Mary stepped into the hallway to make the call, Al turned to Sam, his expression a mix of determination and concern.

"I really hope the Berry's can help us, Sam," he said quietly, his voice heavy with emotion. "Every day that Duncan is allowed to continue his schemes, more innocent people are getting hurt."

Sam placed a comforting hand on his friend's shoulder, his own face etched with empathy. "I know, Al. We're fighting for the truth, for justice. And with Mary's help and the support of people like Lucy, God has shown me we can do this."

Just then, Mary returned, a triumphant smile on her face.

"Great news, guys! The Berry's are more than willing to meet with us. They've invited us over to their house this evening around six."

Sam and Al exchanged a look of pure relief and gratitude. "Mary, you're amazing," Sam said, his voice filled with warmth and admiration. "Thank you so much for arranging this. It means more than you know."

Mary waved off the compliment, but her eyes shone with pleasure. "I'm just happy I could help. Now, let's take a few minutes to prepare some questions for the Berry's. We need to make sure we cover all the important bases."

The three of them huddled together, their voices low and intense as they discussed their approach. Sam could feel the adrenaline coursing through his veins, the thrill of knowing they were one step closer to exposing Duncan for who he truly is.

As the day wore on, the anticipation grew. Sam and Al found themselves pacing the living room, their minds racing with possibilities and scenarios. Mary watched them with a mix of amusement and understanding, her own heart filled with a fierce pride in their dedication and courage.

Finally, the hour of the meeting arrived. As they prepared to leave, Mary pulled Sam and Al into a tight embrace, her voice thick with emotion.

"I know God will guide and protect you every step of the way."

"Thank you, Mary," Sam said, his own voice choked with feeling. "Your love is priceless."

With a final squeeze, they parted, ready to face whatever lay ahead. As they drove to the Berry's' house, Sam and Al felt a sense of calm settle over them, a deep knowing that they were exactly where they were meant to be.

The North Star in the clear evening sky began glimmering, Sam smiled. 'Perfect' he thought to himself. 'God is watching over us.' As they approached the door, he knew that whatever the evening held, they would face it together, united in their quest for truth and their commitment to making the world a better, safer place for all.

Moments later, they approached the quaint cottage that Marion and Don called home. The house was a picture of comfort and warmth, with a well-tended garden out front and a cheerful red door that seemed to beckon them inside.

Mary reached out and knocked, a smile playing at the corners of her mouth as she turned to her companions.

"I have a good feeling about this," she said softly, her eyes sparkling with hope. "I truly believe that Marion and Don will be the key to unlocking the truth about Duncan."

Sam nodded, his own expression one of quiet determination. "I agree, Mary. There's something about this place, about the Berry's... I can feel God's presence here, guiding us forward."

Just then, the door swung open, revealing a woman in her early 40s with a kind, welcoming face. Marion Berry was the picture of a devoted Christian wife and mother, her auburn hair pulled back in a neat bun and her hazel eyes filled with a gentle warmth.

"You must be Sam, Al, and Mary," she said, her voice soft and melodic. "Please, come in. Don and I have been looking forward to meeting you all."

As they stepped inside, Marion ushered them into a cozy living room, where a man with greying hair and a neatly trimmed beard rose to greet them. Don Berry had the look of a man who had weathered many storms, but whose faith had never wavered.

"Welcome," he said, his voice deep and resonant. "We cannot begin to express our gratitude for your willingness to help us in this difficult time."

Sam stepped forward, clasping Don's hand in a firm shake. "It's our honour to be here, Don. Lucy has spoken so highly of you and Marion, and we know that your experiences with Duncan will be so helpful to us in our fight against his deception."

As they settled into the comfortable chairs and sofas, Marion and Don began to share their story, their voices trembling with emotion as they recounted the fear, manipulation, and despair they had endured under Duncan's influence.

"It started out so innocently," Marion said, her eyes distant as she recalled those early days. "We were drawn in by his charisma, his seeming ability to sense our deepest desires and fears. But as time went on, we began to realize that his gifts were nothing more than clever tricks and mind games."

Don nodded, his jaw clenched with anger.

"But he began to demand more and more from us, money, loyalty, obedience.

And if we ever dared to question him or resist his demands, the consequences were... severe."

Sam leaned forward, his expression a mix of compassion and determination. "Marion, Don, I want you to know that you're not alone in this. Al and I have seen firsthand how manipulative and intimidating Duncan can be."

Al nodded, his voice filled with quiet anger.

"He's a fraud, a con man who preys on the vulnerable. But we're here to put an end to his schemes, once and for all."

Marion's eyes filled with tears, her hands trembling as she clasped them together. "You don't know how much it means to us to hear you say that. We've felt so trapped, so helpless for so long."

Don reached over and took his wife's hand, his own voice choked with emotion.

"Marion has been through hell because of Duncan. She... she almost gave up, almost lost hope entirely."

Sam felt his heart clench at the pain in Don's voice. He reached out and placed a comforting hand on the older man's shoulder. "But she didn't give up," he said softly. "And neither did you. You held on, you kept fighting. And now, we're here to fight alongside you."

Marion smiled through her tears, her face filled with a tentative hope. "When Mary called, it felt like an answer to our prayers. Like God was finally sending us the help we so desperately needed."

As the conversation continued, Mary found herself watching Sam, marvelling at the way he seemed to radiate a quiet strength and wisdom beyond his years. She knew that he was deeply attuned to the voice of God, that his faith and his intuition were guiding him forward on this path. And as she listened to Al's unwavering support and loyalty, she felt a swell of pride and affection for these two remarkable men. They were true warriors for Christ, willing to put themselves on the line to protect the vulnerable and defend the truth.

The evening wore on and the group began to discuss their plans for confronting Duncan, their voices rising with excitement and purpose. Sam proposed a bold and daring approach, a direct confrontation, in which they would call out Duncan's lies and manipulations in front of everyone.

Marion and Don exchanged a glance, their faces a mix of fear and hope.

"It's a risky plan," Don said slowly, his brow furrowed in thought. "Duncan will not go down without a fight, and he has many loyal followers who may not take kindly to our accusations."

But Sam was undeterred, his eyes shining with a fierce determination. "I understand the risks," he said, his voice calm and steady. "But I also know that this is what God is calling us to do. We must be willing to stand up for what is right, no matter the cost."

Mary nodded, a slow smile spreading across her face. "I agree with Sam," she said, her voice filled with a quiet strength. "And I think I know the perfect place for this confrontation to take place - Lucy's house. She has a large garden area, plenty of space for a gathering. And with the four of us there as witnesses, Duncan will have nowhere to hide."

As the plan began to take shape, Marion and Don felt a flicker of hope begin to bloom in their hearts. For so long, they had felt trapped and alone, powerless against Duncan's manipulation and control. But now, with Sam, Al, and Mary by their side, they knew that they had a chance to break free, to reclaim their lives and their identity.

The evening drew to a close, Sam, Al, and Mary rose to take their leave, they embraced Marion and Don, their voices thick with emotion as they thanked the couple for their bravery and their trust.

"We will not let you down," Sam promised, his hand resting on Don's shoulder in a gesture of solidarity and support. "Together, we will bring Duncan to justice and free all those who have suffered under his tyranny."

And as they stepped out into the cool night air, the North Star twinkling overhead like a great beacon of hope, they knew that they were ready for whatever lay ahead. With God as their guide and their bond of friendship and faith as their strength, they would face the darkness head-on.

The November twilight wrapped around Mary's cottage like a prayer shawl, while the North Star emerged bright and steady above bare trees. Inside, lamplight created pools of warmth against gathering darkness.

"I'll put the kettle on," Mary called from her kitchen, china clinking. "Earl Grey for you both? And I think there's some of that fruit cake left."

"You spoil us, Mary," Al said warmly, settling into his usual armchair. "Though I suspect we'll need the nutrition for tomorrow."

Sam stood by the window, watching the North Star strengthen. "God's timing is perfect," he murmured. "Even in this."

"Always is," Mary laughed, returning with a laden tea tray. "Though I must admit, my heart's racing just thinking about the impending confrontation."

The phone's sharp ring made them all start. Mary hurried to answer, her free hand clutching her cross.

"Lucy?" she said anxiously. "What news?" Her expression shifted as she listened. "Hold on, let me tell the others." She covered the mouthpiece. "The soothsayer's agreed to meet tomorrow at 4:30. Lucy had to promise potential investors - said it was the only way."

"Classic bait," Al observed grimly. "Money's always their weakness."

Sam nodded, divine certainty filling his voice.

"We'll be there with you, Lucy," Mary said into the phone. "Yes... yes, all three of us. Sam says..." She smiled at his raised eyebrow. "Well, you know how he knows things. Trust him on this."

After she hung up, Sam touched his cross, feeling its familiar warmth. "I'll take the lead tomorrow," he said quietly. "The Spirit's already showing me how this will unfold."

"Your gift never fails to amaze me," Mary said, passing him a fresh cup of tea. "How do you see it playing out?"

"Not easily," he admitted, meeting her concerned gaze. "Men like this soothsayer, they're proud. When their deception's exposed..."

"They lash out," Al finished. "I've seen it in my pastoral work. False prophets hate nothing more than true light."

"Which is exactly what you two bring," Mary said firmly. "Remember how God used you with Iris and Joe Horton?"

Sam smiled at the memory. "Different wolf, same shepherd's staff. Speaking of which, how should we time tomorrow?"

"We'll take my car as usual," suggested Mary. "The question is, should we arrive early before the con man turns up, or go in just after he's arrived?"

Sam knew the answer,

"Let's be there ten minutes beforehand, making sure we're ready for him. He'll be on time. He's so punctual."

"I've no doubt, he'll be punctual," Al agreed. "Types like him always are. Can't resist showing their 'professional' credentials."

"What do you think he will do, Sam?" Mary asked.

"Good question. I think it could get a little hairy, knowing the soothsayer as we do. His temperament is going to be aggressive. So, as I've said before, I'll play it by ear," Sam replied.

Mary set down her teacup with a slight rattle. "I'll be praying the whole time, you know."

"That's where the real battle will be fought anyway," Sam said softly. "In the spiritual realm first, then the physical."

"Ephesians 6:12," Al quoted. "'*For we wrestle not against flesh and blood, but against principalities, against powers...*'"

"'*Against the rulers of the darkness of this world,*'" Sam finished. "But God's light always prevails."

They prayed together one final time, voices joining in quiet harmony. Through the window, the North Star blazed brighter still. Whatever tomorrow's confrontation might bring, they would face it united in divine purpose, armed with truth against Duncan's deception.

Lucy's winter garden dipped in the gathering dusk. Frost sparkled on dormant rosebushes while the North Star emerged early, blazing with unusual brightness. Five crystal glasses of orange juice caught the last sunlight, arranged with careful precision on the garden table.

"Everything's ready," Lucy said, nervously adjusting the glasses. "Though I wish..."

"God's timing is perfect," Sam assured her gently, touching his cross. "Right, Al?"

"Always is," Al agreed, his pastoral calm steadying them all. "Mary, you've got the documents ready?"

Mary patted her handbag. "Every false prophecy, every victim's statement. Though after your vision, Sam, I suspect we won't need them."

The garden gate's click at exactly 4:30 made them all start. Duncan swept in like a stage magician, his expensive camel hair coat and gold rings speaking of profitable deception.

"My potential investors!" he proclaimed, Scottish burr thick with false warmth. "All gathered with full purses, I trust?" His eyes gleamed with predatory assessment.

"Actually, Duncan," Sam said quietly, divine purpose strengthening his voice, "we'd like to discuss how you earn your money."

The soothsayer's practiced smile flickered. "Careful now, laddie," he growled, facade cracking. "You're paddling in deep waters here. I came for investment, not interrogation."

"We know about the false prophecies," Sam pressed. "The 'cosmic revelations' you sell to vulnerable souls. The 'curses' you claim to lift, for a price."

"You dare?" Duncan's mask shattered completely. His face contorted with rage. "You'll regret this interference, boy! I'll give you a right trouncing. It's you that's in for it. I'm coming over to you. I'm going to pummel you. You'll need a hospital when I've finished with you." He moved with surprising speed for his bulk, launching himself at Sam. But two years of amateur boxing had prepared Sam for just such divine purpose. As Duncan's wild right hook came, Sam slipped it smoothly, years of ring training taking over.

"God's truth prevails," Sam said quietly, delivering a precise counter that carried heaven's judgment. The sound of knuckles meeting jaw echoed through the garden like thunder. Duncan crashed to the frost-hardened ground, scrambling up to flee with both pride and face badly bruised.

"This isn't over!" he shouted, but fear had replaced rage in his voice as he bolted out of the garden. The gate slammed shut behind him.

"Good Lord," Lucy breathed, gripping her chair for support. Al moved quickly to steady her.

Seeing Lucy's reaction, Mary exclaimed. "I think we will need something warmer than orange juice," she suggested, making her way into the kitchen. Moments later she reappeared. "Tea," she announced firmly, though her hands shook slightly. "Strong tea, with plenty of sugar. We all need some after that."

Over steaming cups, they processed what had happened.

"I've never..." Lucy began, then stopped. "Well, I never expected quite such a dramatic confrontation."

"Sometimes light has to be quite direct with darkness," Al said quietly, wisdom evident in his tone.

"God's light always prevails," Sam added, rubbing his knuckles thoughtfully. "Though I suspect this battle isn't quite finished."

"Tomorrow then," Mary suggested, pouring more tea. "Tomorrow you can pay him a visit. Give him time to feel the full weight of today's... revelation."

"Agreed," Al nodded. "Sometimes defeat needs time to become redemption. Though perhaps we should ice those knuckles first, Sam?"

The North Star blazed brighter as they planned their next move, divine confirmation lighting their path forward. Another wolf had been confronted, now they needed to ensure the flock stayed safe.

The November morning wrapped the street in crystalline silence as Sam and Al approached Duncan's house. Their footsteps cracked through frost like breaking glass, while the North Star, though faint in daylight, guided their purpose.

"Quite a respectable neighbourhood," Al observed, looking at the well-kept gardens. "Perfect cover for his deceptions."

"Appearances were his speciality," Sam added, pulling his coat tighter. "Everything for show." He felt divine guidance strengthen as Al's knock echoed unanswered through the house.

Moments later a neighbour emerged, keys jangling.

"Looking for Duncan?" the man asked, studying them with shrewd eyes. "You're too late. Left yesterday in quite a state - face swollen something fierce." He held up the keys meaningfully. "Asked me to give these to the landlord."

"Heading back to Scotland, is he?" Sam asked carefully, though the Spirit had already revealed the truth.

The neighbour's laugh held no humour. "Scotland? That was just part of his act, like those fancy 'cosmic visions' he was always on about. Spent maybe a year there and picked up the accent. He's southern-born, though good luck getting any truth from him. Kept everything close to his chest, that one."

"Never trusted him myself," he added, jingling the keys thoughtfully. "Something off about him, like he was always performing."

"The best con men usually are," Al said softly, pastoral experience evident in his tone.

"Thank you," Sam said, the feeling of satisfaction flowed through his body. "You've helped more than you know."

Mary's kitchen welcomed them back with warmth and familiar comfort when they returned. Steam rose from her best china cups as they settled around the well-worn table, their mission's completion settling over them like a blessing.

"I'll need to contact Pastor James," Mary said, pouring tea with careful precision. "And those poor souls Duncan deceived - they need to hear the truth before rumours start flying." Her hands trembled slightly. "Though I hardly know how I'll manage once you've gone. This house will feel so empty..." She paused for a moment, "The weather's turning colder," she added quickly, trying to mask her emotion. "Are you certain about leaving today?"

Sam reached across to squeeze her hand, feeling both her affection and her grief. "We must answer God's calling, Mary and go where he takes us. Even when it aches. Leaving you won't be easy but I sense God is calling us back to the canal path to follow the North Star"

"You've become like family," Al added, sensing the emotion Mary was trying to hide. "This house has been more than just shelter."

"It's been a base for God's work," Mary said firmly, though her eyes glistened. "First Iris, then Joe Horton, and then Duncan. He's used you both so powerfully."

Sam smiled gently. "He used all of us, Mary. Your concerns started our work. Your home became holy ground for planning His purpose."

"And your tea kept us going through it all," Al added, trying to lighten the mood. Mary gave a watery chuckle.

As they gathered their few possessions, worn Bibles, spare clothes, the essentials of their calling, Mary pressed packages into their hands.

"Sandwiches for the journey," she explained. "And I've put some fruit cake in too. The kind Al likes."

"Mary..." Sam began, but she shook her head.

"Let me do this much," she insisted. "And promise you'll come back when

He leads you this way again."

"Count on it," Al assured her, hugging her close. "You're part of our journey now."

At the door, Mary's composure finally broke. "Be careful out there," she whispered. "Let the Star guide you true."

"We always will," Sam said softly, embracing her. "God has never failed us yet."

They walked away down the frost-covered path, Mary's figure growing smaller behind them. The North Star, though hidden by morning light, pulled them toward the canal where their journey had begun.

"She's a blessing," Al said quietly as they walked. "A true servant of God."

"More than that," Sam replied, touching his cross. "She's proof that divine appointments work both ways. We needed her as much as our new friends needed us."

The canal path opened before them, a familiar yet promising new adventure. Ahead, the Navvy Bridge waited like a gateway to their next calling. Behind them, Mary's last words carried on the winter wind:

"Go with God, dear friends. Go with God."

I speak the name of Jesus

CHAPTER 8

CAN YOU HEAR THAT?

The canal path welcomed Sam and Al like an old friend, frost sparkling on bare branches while the North Star, though faint in morning light, guided their steps. Winter birds called from skeletal trees, their song mixing with the soft lap of water against the bank.

"Strange to be back here," Al said softly, adjusting his pack. "Where it all began."

Sam touched his cross, feeling divine warmth pulse through it. "We are exactly where God wants us to be Al."

"Iris, Joe Horton, Duncan..." Al shook his head in wonder. "Who do you think He'll send us to next?"

"We'll know when..." Sam's voice trailed off as he spotted a figure in the distance, moving toward them. His divine guidance strengthened immediately. "Al, look ahead. About two hundred meters."

Al squinted against the morning light. "I see him. There is something about his walk, Sam..."

"He's been searching for us," Sam said with quiet certainty. "God's led him here. This is what God is telling me, Al."

They watched as the man approached, and then suddenly he veered down the embankment.

"Careful," Al cautioned as they hurried to the spot. "He seems skittish."

At the bottom of the slope stood a man in his thirties, shoulders hunched against more than just the cold. His clothes, though clean, spoke of someone trying to fade into backgrounds.

"Hi there," Sam called gently. "I'm Sam, this is Al. We'd love to talk if you're willing."

Silence stretched for a moment before the man spoke.

"I knew you were the ones," he said softly. "I've been watching, waiting... People call me Tricky Smart."

"Because you're clever at staying unnoticed?" Sam asked, divine insight guiding his words.

Tricky's eyes widened with surprise. "How did...? Yes, exactly that. I observe everything and understand more than most. But it's made me... different. Apart. I've always been a loner. My mates were okay with me until they got their girlfriends. I used to still knock around with them, but I was always the gooseberry. Eventually, all my mates got married. I had trouble attracting a girlfriend, so I drifted away from my friends." He paused for a moment, wondering if he should continue expaining.

Sam and Al remained silent, they wanted to hear his story.

So, that's where I am now. There is so much I've missed." Tricky continued. "I have lots of things I need to catch up on. I want to get my life back on track. I've been attending a local church not far from here, hoping Jesus would reach out and lift me up and set me on the right track."

"Would you share your real name?" Sam asked gently. "The one God knows you by?"

Something shifted in the man's face - hope warring with fear of trust. "John," he whispered. "John Jones. I haven't heard anyone call me that in years."

Suddenly, a cry echoed across the water: "Ahoy there!"

They all started, looking around.

"That happens sometimes," John explained. "No one knows who..."

"Ahoy there!" The mysterious call came again, seeming to bounce between water and sky.

"A message, maybe," Sam mused, touching his cross in his pocket. "Someone else who needs finding?"

John's face lit with unexpected animation. "Speaking of finding people, you know the Francis sisters? Marg and Coolness? They talk about you at our church when they visit their Aunt Kalisa. Would you...would you come tonight? To our meeting? You You could meet up with the Francis sisters again and meet our Pastor, Pastor Bill will be there. He's always there."

Sam felt divine confirmation surge through him. "What time?"

"Six-thirty," John said eagerly. "I live with my mum, she's part of the fellowship too. She's been praying I'd find... friends. Real ones."

"Ahoy there!" The cry echoed once more, but this time it seemed almost joyful.

"God works in mysterious ways," Sam said softly, smiling, as they helped John back up the embankment. "Even through mysterious voices."

The Pentecostal church rose against the November night like a lighthouse, its stained-glass windows glowing with warmth and welcome. Sam felt God's divine guidance with each step toward the entrance, his cross pulsing warm inside his pocket. The North Star shone directly above the spire, as if marking holy ground.

Inside the minor hall, the atmosphere buzzed with spiritual energy. Pastor Bill hurried to meet them, his face radiant with divine joy.

"Thank the Lord you've come," he said, gripping their hands warmly. "Mark told me how God used you with Joe Horton. And now..." He glanced meaningfully at John. "The Francis sisters spoke of you often," he added, eyes twinkling. "They told me how God works through you, Sam."

Before Sam could respond, excited voices called out.

"Sam! Al!" Marg and Coolness hurried over, their faces glowing with recognition. The sisters embraced them like a long-lost family.

"We've been praying you'd come," Coolness said, keeping hold of their hands. "Can you come and stay with us at Aunty Kalisa's? She has a room ready for you both - said she knew in her spirit God would guide you both here."

"God's plan in action," Sam replied softly, divine confirmation flooding through him. "We need to help John find his way back."

Pastor Bill turned to John, laying a fatherly hand on his shoulder. "Brother

John," he said deliberately, emphasizing the name. "Not Tricky anymore, praise God. He's sent you true shepherds to guide you home."

John's eyes filled with tears. "I feel it, Pastor. For the first time in so long, I feel... seen. Really seen."

The service flowed with Holy Spirit power, worship rising like incense to heaven. When Pastor Bill introduced them, the congregation's welcome felt like a divine embrace. Sam watched John during the prayers, seeing tension melt from his shoulders as fellowship wrapped around him like a warm blanket

Afterwards, the miracle of connection unfolded before them. A church member approached John naturally, without prompting.

"Need a lift home, mate? I'm heading that way."

John's face transformed with surprised joy. "Thanks," he managed, wonder in his voice. "That's... that's really kind."

As Sam and Al walked to the car park with Marg and Coolness they heard the mysterious cry pierced the night:

"Ahoy there!"

Al scanned the darkness, puzzled.

"There it is again. Following us, do you think?"

"Or guiding us," Sam said thoughtfully, touching his cross. He knew this mysterious voice was part of God's unfolding plan. The North Star blazed above them as they drove towards Aunty Kalisa's house. This mission was more than just helping John, he sensed. God was weaving together threads they couldn't yet see into a tapestry of divine purpose.

Aunty Kalisa's Victorian cottage stood like a lighthouse against the November darkness, its windows glowing with welcome. Inside, warmth wrapped around them like a prayer blanket, while the scent of fresh-baked bread and brewing tea spoke of home. Sam looked up out of the window, seeing The North Star shine through the diamond-paned windows, blessing this new sanctuary.

"Aunty," Marg's voice held pride and nervous hope. "These are our dear friends Sam and Al. The ones we told you about." She twisted her hands slightly. "Could they stay while they help John find his way back?"

Aunty Kalisa moved with the grace of years spent in ministry. Her silver hair caught lamplight like a crown as she embraced them both without hesitation.

"My distinguished guests!" Joy radiated from her face. "The Spirit told me to prepare the spare room days ago."

Sam felt his cross pulse warm with confirmation. Al's pastoral experience showed in his gentle smile, they both recognized a fellow servant of God.

"Come, come, please make yourself at home. I will go and make us all some tea." Aunty gestured toward her kitchen, where copper pots gleamed in firelight. "Tea first, then we'll talk of tomorrow's work. Marg, will you help me with the tea?"

Marg nodded, following Aunty into the kitchen.

Aunty Kalisa's sitting room wrapped them in Victorian elegance as evening settled outside. Cream and gold wallpaper caught lamplight in its subtle pattern of roses, while deep burgundy curtains framed diamond-paned windows where the North Star shone brightly. Family photographs in silver frames covered every surface, a testament to decades of ministry and love. The old fireplace, its mantlepiece carved with grape vines, held pride of place, while comfortable armchairs arranged around it spoke of countless hours of prayer and fellowship.

The sound of Aunty and Marg bustling about with cups and saucers could be heard in the background, as Sam, Al and Coolness relaxed in the comfy chairs.

Coolness leaned forward eagerly. "What's your vision for helping John?" Her experience as a social worker was evident in her concern.

Sam touched his cross, seeking guidance.

"Integration first," he said thoughtfully. "He needs to feel truly part of the body of Christ. Bible study to feed his spirit, sharing the Gospel to light his path. Baptism will come when the Spirit leads him there."

Marg and Aunty appeared bearing a tray laden with love, fresh bread, local honey, cheese from the market. As they shared this simple feast, Sam felt divine purpose settling over them like a benediction.

"We can help," Coolness nodded, exchanging looks with Marg. "Our work in care and social welfare..." She glanced across at Aunty. "And Aunty's gift for spiritual healing..."

"John's mother?" Sam asked, wanting to know more. "Have you met her?

What is she like?"

"Mel! Oh she's amazing," Coolness's face softened. "Strong in faith, despite everything. She's been John's anchor through his darkest times. He may have lost his way, but he never lost his respect for her."

Sam saw God's plan unfolding in front of him. "Could you arrange a visit? We should organise a bible study with both of them?"

"Sure, that's no problem, I will go and call her now," replied Coolness standing. She moved swiftly across the lounge, and out into the hallway.

Ten minutes later, Coolness returned beaming. "Tomorrow after ten," she announced. "Mel almost cried with joy when I mentioned you coming."

"How far away is their house?" Al asked practically, always mindful of logistics.

"Oh, it's only about ten minutes along the canal path," she explained.

'God's path,' Sam thought silently to himself with a smile. *'The canal path is the path of His light.'*

The hours ticked by and soon it was time for bed. Thanking Aunty for the wonderful meal and being such a warm host, Sam and Al followed her upstairs as she showed them the spare room where they would be sleeping.

"You should be quite comfortable in here my friends, although, you may need to open the window slightly for ventilation, - the room gets very warm when the heating is on. God bless you both and may he keep you safe through the night." She said, her tone expressing a gratitude of warmth for the arrival of her guests. "See you at breakfast."

Al sat down on one of the single beds. "She's right about how warm it is in here," he commented, feeling the heat. "Let's open the window, just a bit Sam, for some cool air."

Sam nodded; he prised open the window ever so slightly. "There that should do it." A faint breeze caught the lace net curtain as it drifted in through the window. Suddenly, the mysterious cry found them even there, floating through the evening air:

"Ahoy there!"

"Following us still," Al observed, arranging his well-worn Bible on the bedside table.

"Leading us," Sam corrected gently, touching his cross. Tomorrow they would begin their real work, helping John navigate from darkness into light, from isolation into God's family.

Outside their window, the North Star blazed steady and bright, while inside, Aunty Kalisa's house held them in its prayer-soaked peace. The perfect base for a divine purpose to unfold.

The evening sunlight painted Mel's garden in pearl and gold as Sam and Al approached her house. Frost sparkled on winter roses while the North Star remained faintly visible, guiding their steps. Just as Sam's hand reached for the doorbell, that mysterious voice rang out with startling clarity:

"Ahoy there, me hearties!"

"Closer than ever," Sam murmured, his cross pulsating with warmth and divine significance. "Almost as if it's right behind us..."

Before Al could reply, his thoughtful response was interrupted by the loud melodious chime echoing through Mel's house. The door opened immediately, releasing warmth and the scent of fresh coffee. Mel stood framed in the doorway; her face radiant with the kind of hope only faith can bring.

"Welcome, welcome," she beamed, gesturing them inside. "John's been up since dawn, reading his Bible. He's so eager to begin."

The living room breathed years of family prayers. Well-worn Bibles waited on a polished table while reflecting light from the gleaming North Star shone through lace curtains casting patterns like church windows on the floor. John sat straight-backed, alert - transformation already visible in his posture.

"Shall we begin with Mark?" Sam suggested, divine guidance clear as crystal. He opened his Bible. "John, would you read for us? Verses one through eight?"

John's voice, once hesitant, now carried strength and understanding. The words of scripture flowed through him like living water. When he finished, Al leaned forward, pastoral instincts noting every change.

"What speaks to your heart there, John?"

"Isaiah's prophecy," John replied without hesitation, his eyes bright with holy fire. "The messenger, John the Baptist, preparing the way. But it's more than that..." He paused, choosing words carefully. "It's about transformation - water baptism pointing toward Spirit baptism through Jesus. Like... just like what's happening to me now."

Sam felt divine confirmation surge through him. "You've studied deeply," he observed, catching Mel's gaze.

"We used to study weekly," she said softly, mother's pride warring with old pain. "Before..." Her words trailed off.

"Before I lost my way," he finished gently. "But God never lost me, did He?"

Moving to Mark 9:35, they watched John grasp ever-deeper truths.

John cleared his throat. "Being last to put others first," he explained, passion growing. "The Spirit creating humility in us... it's beautiful, really. Jesus said, 'He who wants to be first must be last and servant of all.' The Holy Spirit creates a desire in us to be in last place so others can be first in God's Kingdom too!"

"You're finding yourself again," Sam said quietly, pride reflecting in his tone. "Clean inside, showing outside. This isn't just change, John - it's restoration. God returning you to who He always meant you to be."

Mel's eyes filled with tears.

"I thought I'd lost him forever," she whispered, reaching for John's hand. "But God sent you both... it's miracle after miracle."

The North Star shone visibly as they prepared to leave, blessing this holy moment of healing. As they walked away, that mysterious voice called once more across the frost-bright garden:

"Ahoy there!"

"It's getting clearer every time," Al observed thoughtfully. "Like it's drawing closer to us."

"Like everything else," Sam replied, touching his cross in his pocket. The warmth there suggested their work with John was just beginning, another thread in God's greater tapestry.

Back at Aunty's house, as Sam and Al made themselves comfortable. Aunty, Coolness and Marg were eager to know how their bible study with Mel and John went.

Coolness perched on the edge of her chair, hardly able to contain herself. Her colourful dress made a bright contrast to the room's muted tones.

"Please," she burst out, "don't keep us in suspense! How did it go with John?"

"Let them catch their breath first," Aunty chided gently, adjusting a crocheted antimacassar on her chair's arm. "Tea before testimony."

"No, no," Sam smiled, settling into the deep leather armchair that had already become his favourite. "John's transformation deserves immediate sharing."

"The Spirit's work in him is profound," Al added, choosing his words carefully as he sat straighter in his chair. "His grasp of scripture, his hunger for truth..."

"Mel taught him better than she knew," Sam continued, watching hope bloom on their faces. "The foundation was always there, just buried for a time. Now..." He gestured expressively. "Now he's not just reading scripture, - he's living it."

"Praise Jesus!" Coolness exclaimed, actually bouncing in her seat. Marg reached over to squeeze her sister's hand, tears of joy tracking down her cheeks.

"Another soul restored," Aunty Kalisa said softly, her eyes distant with the memory of other victories.

"You'll stay?" Marg asked suddenly, leaning forward in her floral wingback chair. "Please? There are others..." She glanced at Coolness meaningfully.

Sam felt divine confirmation pulse through him. "Where God leads," he said warmly, meeting Al's knowing look.

"After dinner then," Aunty decided, rising with practiced grace. "We'll discuss what's next over my shepherd's pie."

When they had finished dinner, and all the dishes had been washed and neatly put away, they sat back down together in the sitting room, the room felt different - charged with holy purpose. Coolness stood by the fireplace, her professional demeanour replacing earlier excitement.

"It's our friend Amari," she began, twisting her silver cross necklace. "She works with Marg at the care home. Depression and anxiety have her in their grip, and..." She paused, choosing her words carefully. "There's something deeper there. Something she's carrying alone."

"The root's always key," Sam said gently. "But prayer comes first. It's up to each one of us to commit to prayer and supplication for her and involve Amari. She should do the same, prayer and supplication. So, we are all on the same hymn sheet."

"I agree," Al responded, clear, his tone supportive of Sam's words. "We will also need to have an informal chat with Amari. Can you arrange this Coolness for us please?"

Coolness nodded without hestitation, "I will go and call her now." Her call to Amari felt Spirit-led, each word falling perfectly into place. Returning back into the sitting room, she smiled at Sam and Al, "Tomorrow at ten," she announced, relief bright in her voice.

"Will you be accompanying us Coolness? Quizzed Al, thinking it would be much better if she and Marg could.

"Yes, we'll come. I think Amari will feel more comfortable if we are there with you. I'll drive us there. It's not far but just in case its raining."

"Let's give thanks to Jesus in prayer and meditation," suggested Sam, bowing his head to begin. "Heavenly Father, we come together to give thanks for your love, guidance and protection. We thank you for the blessing of patience and understanding. May we take the healing of the Holy Spirit to Amari, - so she may heal and find joy in your light. Amen."

"Amen," the group chorused.

Tomorrow would bring new challenges, but tonight they could rest in the joy of John's restoration while preparing their hearts for Amari's healing. The North Star blazed brighter through the burgundy curtains, blessing their holy purpose.

Morning light filtered through Aunty Kalisa's lace curtains, turning the sitting room's shade into a glimmering pearl, as they gathered for morning prayer.

"No one leaves this house unfed," Aunty announced, her flowered dressing gown sweeping regally toward her kitchen. "Especially not before important work."

Coolness couldn't keep still her bright yellow dress a splash of sunshine as she paced. "You need to understand this about Amari," she began, stopping to straighten a photo of her mother. "She's remarkable, really."

"Tell us everything," Sam encouraged, settling into the comfy leather armchair.

"She came from Lagos five years ago," Marg began, curled in her usual corner of the floral settee. "Top of her nursing class there. But something's changed these past months."

"The joy's gone," Coolness added, sinking finally into a chair. "She still serves everyone else - that's her way. But her eyes..." She twisted her silver cross necklace. "They've lost their light."

"Sometimes the strongest believers carry the heaviest burdens," Al observed quietly, understanding in his tone. "Especially when far from home."

"Because they think they should bear them alone," Aunty observed, returning with a laden tea tray. Steam rose from her best china cups like morning prayers."Especially for those used to being strong for others."

"That's it exactly," Coolness exclaimed. "She's tall, elegant, carries herself like a queen, really. Always perfectly dressed, not a hair out of place in her braids. But lately..."

"The facade's cracking?" Sam suggested gently, his divine insight growing stronger. "We'll need to listen with our hearts when we meet her."

"Yes! She lives in that lovely Victorian terrace on Chapel Lane," Marg added. "Keeps her house like a showpiece, African art mixed with English antiques. Everything perfect, everything controlled..."

"Pride," Sam murmured, touching his cross. "That might be part of what we need to understand."

"We should leave soon," Coolness said, checking her watch. "Amari's precisely punctual - it matters to her, being more 'professional' than anyone expects."

"Another weight she carries," Sam said softly, divine understanding growing. "Being perfect for everyone."

"You'll help her?" Marg asked anxiously. "Help her find joy again?"

"God will," Sam assured her, feeling his cross warm in confirmation. "We're just His instruments." He paused thoughtfully for a moment. "We are here just following God's path," he added, understanding the path ahead.

They finished their tea in thoughtful silence, each preparing their heart for the work ahead. Through the window, the last glimpse of the North Star blessed their purpose - another soul needing God's light, another divine appointment on their continuing journey.

The morning sunlight blessed Amari's Victorian terrace, its red brick glowing like sacred fire. The front garden showed her perfectionist nature - every plant was precisely trimmed, even in winter dormancy. As they approached along the slate path, bordered by sleeping lavender, that mysterious voice rang out with startling clarity:

"Ahoy there, me hearties!"

"Closer than ever," Sam murmured, his cross pulsating in his pocket. "Like it's watching over us."

"We hear it often," Coolness explained, adjusting her bright yellow head wrap. "But never quite this clear."

The door opened before they could knock, revealing Amari in her full grace, tall and elegant in a traditional blue Ankara dress, its patterns speaking of home and heritage. Her braids were woven into an intricate crown. Her sitting room told two stories at once. Nigerian artwork, masks wearing centuries of wisdom, carved figures dancing with ancient joy stood in perfect harmony with Victorian antiques. Hand-woven textiles in earth tones draped Queen Anne chairs, while delicate English bone china waited on a coffee table of deep mahogany. Everything gleamed with almost desperate perfection.

"Welcome, dear friends," Amari's Lagos accent carried warmth beneath strain. "Please, make yourselves comfortable." She gestured to the carefully arranged chairs.

"Your home is beautiful," Al said gently, noting how she straightened an already perfect cushion. "Such wonderful blending of cultures."

"Like heaven's gathering," Coolness added warmly. "All nations together in harmony."

Sam felt divine guidance strengthen as they settled into chairs. "Tell us what's burdening your heart, sister."

Amari's careful composure cracked slightly. Her fingers worked the edge of a woven throw. "It's work," she began hesitantly. "One person - Jean Simpson. She..." Her voice caught as professional pride warred with pain. "She constantly undermines me and makes me feel small. Like I'm not qualified enough, not English enough. I cry at night now, wondering why..." ..." A tear escaped despite her rigid control.

"Oh, sweet sister," Coolness breathed, reaching for her hand.

"We need to pray for Jean," Sam said gently, his cross warming further. "And for you. Sometimes those who hurt others are hurting deeply themselves."

"The strongest attack often comes from the most wounded," Al added, wisdom in his tone. "Smile at her. Show her God's love through you, it may be love she's never known. She may be fighting battles we don't know about"

They bowed heads together, African and English voices joining in silent supplication. The room seemed to hold its breath for fifteen holy minutes until Sam felt divine confirmation.

"Amen," he said softly. "How does your heart feel now?" he asked Amari, seeing how her shoulders had finally relaxed.

"Lighter," she admitted, a glimmer of her natural joy returning. "Like a weight is lifting. Like..." She smiled suddenly, transforming her whole face. "Like I'm not alone in this battle anymore."

Sam shared Philippians 4:5-7, watching understanding dawn in her eyes. "A supplication with thanksgiving," he emphasized. "Even... especially, for those who hurt us."

"The fruit will come," Marg assured her, squeezing her hand. "Keep praying, keep showing love. And remember - you have family here."

As they prepared to leave, Amari's smile reached her eyes for the first time. "Thank you," she said softly. "For helping me see God's way forward. I'm ready to work on this new approach with Jean now, - thank you all."

Thanking Amari for her hospitality, they gathered their things together and said their goodbyes. During the drive back to Aunty's house, they gave blessings for this first step in Amari's healing. Another soul moving from darkness toward light, another divine appointment fulfilling God's perfect plan.

Aunty Kalisa's sitting room glowed with evening warmth as they returned. Its cream and gold wallpaper catching the lamplight like captured prayers. She stood waiting by her favourite armchair, silver hair gleaming, hands smoothing her already-pristine lace tablecloth with nervous energy.

"Well?" she burst out, maternal concern overwhelming her usual reserve. "Don't keep me in suspense a moment longer! How's our dear Amari?"

Coolness sank into the floral settee, her yellow dress bright against burgundy upholstery. "Oh Aunty," she began, joy evident in her voice. "You should have seen how the Spirit moved!"

"We prayed together," Sam added quietly, touching his cross which still felt warm from their ministry. "The verses God led us to... they were exactly what she needed."

"Tell me everything," Aunty insisted, perching on her chair's edge. "Every blessed detail."

Al smiled gently. "The hope in her eyes, Aunty, you could actually see the moment God's peace touched her."

"It wasn't just the prayers," Marg added eagerly. "It was seeing her perfect house, understanding how hard she works to prove herself worthy..."

"Ah," Aunty nodded, wisdom deepening her eyes. "Our African sister carries too many burdens. Like I did when I first came here."

"You never told us that story," Coolness said softly, leaning forward.

"Another time, dear. First..." Aunty rose with purpose. "You've done holy work today. That calls for celebration." She disappeared into her kitchen, returning with a laden tray that spoke of love through nourishment. Steam rose from covered dishes like prayers ascending.

"Nigerian jollof rice," she announced proudly. "Made it while you were gone. And..." She unveiled another dish with a flourish. "Traditional Yorkshire puddings. Because heaven's table will have all nations' food!"

They laughed together, the sound like bells of joy. As they ate, Aunty watched them with shining eyes. "You're a blessed team," she said suddenly. "Each of you bringing different gifts to God's work."

"Speaking of gifts," Sam said thoughtfully, "that mysterious voice followed us to Amari's..."

"Did it now!" Aunty exclaimed, crossing herself. "Surely that's a sign?"

"Of what's to come," Sam agreed, feeling blessed. "We are so fortunate to be guided by God."

As the evening continued, they gathered closer around Aunty's fireplace. The flames cast dancing shadows on the walls while outside, the North Star blessed their council through the diamond-paned windows.

"We need to think longer-term," Sam said thoughtfully. "Jean Simpson isn't Amari's only challenge."

Coolness nodded eagerly, setting down her tea cup. "It's about belonging, isn't it? I see it at work, how hard she tries to be 'more English than the English.'"

"Like I did," Aunty said softly, settling deeper into her armchair. "Perhaps... perhaps it is the time I shared my story with you all."

"Would you, Aunty?" Marg looked up from her corner of the settee. "It could mean so much, coming from you."

"When I first came from Jamaica," Aunty began, her eyes distant with memory, "I thought I had to be perfect. Every word pronounced just so, every room spotless, every gesture controlled..."

"Like Amari's house," Al observed gently. "Not a cushion out of place."

"Exactly." Aunty's smile held years of hard-won wisdom. "Until I learned that God loves us in our authenticity, not our perfection."

"That's it!" Sam sat forward suddenly, divine inspiration clear in his voice. "That's what she needs to hear, that she's loved for who she is, not what she achieves."

"We could start a weekly prayer group," Coolness suggested. "Just for immigrant women in the church. A safe place to be real."

"And I'll speak with Pastor Bill," Sam added. "About addressing this need from the pulpit."

Suddenly, that mysterious cry pierced the evening quiet:

"Ahoy there!"

"Our mysterious voice is even in agreement with our plans," Marg laughed softly.

Sam touched his cross, feeling divine confirmation. "This goes beyond Amari now. God's showing us a broader mission."

"Then we'd better get more Yorkshire puddings in," Aunty said practically, though her eyes shone with purpose. "If we're starting a prayer group, we'll need proper nourishment."

They laughed together, the sound mixing with crackling flames like a melody of hope. Outside, the North Star blazed brighter, blessing their expanding mission.

The hours ticked by, unnoticed at first but then Coolness was the first to acknowledge the late hour. "I'm tired," she announced. "I'll turn in for the night."

One by one, they prepared for rest. Goodnights were exchanged - not mere words, but blessings. Promises of continued support. Affirmations of their spiritual connection.

"Well done, everyone," Sam said as they prepared to separate. "Remember, our work with Amari doesn't end here."

Aunty's final words wrapped around them like a spiritual blanket. "The Lord is watching over her," she said softly. "And He's watching over all of us."

Aunty's kitchen glowed with the sunrise, the oak table laden with morning bounty. Steam rose from teacups while toast and eggs waited on Aunty's best china. The North Star faded slowly, blessing their morning council.

"Before we dive into breakfast," Sam began, his tone reflecting the seriousness of his words, "I need to know we're all united in prayer for Amari. The Spirit woke me three times last night, showing me how crucial this unified supplication is."

"Every morning during my garden prayers," Aunty nodded, passing the marmalade. "And every evening before bed. Been asking specifically for Jean's heart to soften."

"I've been praying in tongues over it," Coolness added, her light blue dress bright in the morning light. "And I'll see her Sunday at church. Planning to invite her for lunch after service - she needs to know she has family here."

"That's perfect," Marg reached to squeeze her sister's hand. "You know how she tries to rush off after service like she's afraid to let anyone too close."

"Speaking of transformation," Sam said thoughtfully, buttering his toast, "the Spirit's pressing on my heart about John. We need to check his progress, see how the Bible study's flourishing."

Al nodded eagerly. "Good thinking. His journey could encourage Amari too, showing her how God transforms lives when we let Him in."

"And Mel's technique with Bible study," Sam continued, his divine insight growing stronger. "She might have wisdom for helping Amari ground herself in scripture."

"I'll phone them now," Coolness offered, rising swiftly. "They'll be finished with morning devotions."

Coolness's warm voice could be heard from the hall: "Mel! Yes, it's Coolness. Sam and Al were just talking about John's progress... They would like to visit you both again. Would this evening work? Say six-thirty?"

Suddenly that mysterious voice called through the open kitchen window.

"Ahoy there!"

"Even commenting on our plans now," Al chuckled.

Coolness returned beaming.

"All arranged! Mel sounded so excited to share John's progress."

"God's weaving it all together," Sam said softly, before taking another bite of toast. "Using each story to strengthen the others."

"Then we'd better finish this lovely breakfast," Aunty said practically, though her eyes shone. "Lots of kingdom work ahead today."

Mel's living room glowed, radiating the warmth of restoration. Family photos, once painful reminders of better days, now spoke of hope renewed.

"Welcome, dear ones," Mel's voice trembled with joy as she embraced Sam and Al. "Such a different meeting from last time, all because of God's grace through you." Her eyes glistened as she straightened a cushion. "The change happened so fast, yet so completely."

John stood straighter now, confidence replacing his former shadows. His whole bearing spoke of transformation. "I can hardly believe who I was just weeks ago," he said, emotion making his voice rough. "That lost soul, hiding from everyone... but now?" He gestured to his worn Bible on the coffee table. "Now I'm home - with God, with Mom, with myself."

Sam felt his heart burst with gratitude to God. "Tell us about your studies, John. The Spirit's showing me you've found real depth there."

"The Gospels first," John's face lit with genuine excitement. "Not just reading them, really understanding them. And now Ruth..." He reached for his Bible with reverent familiarity. "Listen to this - 'Where you go, I will go. Where you stay, I will stay. Your people will be my people, and your God my God.'"

"Perfect scripture for today's world," Sam nodded, seeing divine parallels. "When everyone's choosing their own path..."

"Like I was," John added softly. "Until God sent you all."

Mel bustled in to her kitchen, joy making her movements light. "This calls for a proper celebration - my special biscuit selection!" While she prepared tea, Al leaned forward eagerly.

"And church life, John? Are you feeling more connected?"

"It's amazing," John's smile reached his eyes, something they'd never seen before. "Actually looking forward to services now. Thinking about joining the men's group..."

"Oh John! That's wonderful news." Sam exclaimed "If only you could see yourself as I do now, as we all do."

They shared tea and treats, fellowship flowing as naturally as breathing. Later as they prepared to leave, the atmosphere was thick with holy satisfaction. This wasn't just transformation, it was restoration, resurrection, and redemption made visible.

"We'll see you Sunday," Sam said warmly, touching the cross in his pocket in blessing.

Aunty Kalisa's sitting room welcomed them home with golden lamplight and the scent of evening tea. Her face glowed with anticipation as they entered, noting their satisfied expressions.

"Those smiles tell quite a story," she said warmly, patting the sofa beside her. "Tell me everything about John."

Al sank into his favourite chair, his face glowing with pride. "It's more than we dared hope! The transformation..." he clasped her hands together in joy. "It's like seeing a butterfly emerge."

"Complete restoration," Sam added, his cross still felt warm from their visit. "His Bible knowledge runs deep now, you should hear him quote Ruth!"

"Praise His holy name!" Aunty's eyes filled with happy tears. "Now we must keep Amari lifted up in the same way."

"Sunday will tell us more," Sam said thoughtfully. Divine guidance was already showing him connections. Our prayers, along with her prayers and good Christian actions in the workplace, should see some progress in her relationship with Jean."

Al, exhausted from the day's events, felt his eyes wanting to close, stretched out his arms and yawned. "Yawnnnn. It's getting late. I'm going to turn in for the night. Good night, all." He said, yawning again.

"Wait for me. I'm going to hit the pillow as well. It's been a successful but tiring day," said Sam, needing to sleep. "God bless and goodnight, Aunty. We'll see you bright and early in the morning."

The next morning, after breakfast, the five friends came together for group prayer and Bible reading before Coolness and Marg went off to work.

Sam looked out of the kitchen window, seeing the pleasant wintery sun he had an idea.

"How about a nice walk to the park?" He suggested to Al "The fresh air will do us the world of good."

Al thought it was a perfect idea, and he felt in the mood for a nice long stroll. "Sure, that will be great. "Let me get my coat."

The park was only a few minutes' walk away from Aunty's house and soon Sam and Al found themselves at the park. The November sunshine transformed the park into a crystal garden, frost sparkling on every surface like scattered diamonds. Ancient oaks reached bare branches toward the pearl-white sky, their massive trunks dark against the morning light.

"Look how the light catches everything," Al breathed, his breath forming tiny pockets of mist the cold air. "Like God's touching each blade of grass."

Just then, that mysterious voice rang out, clearer than ever in the winter stillness:

"Ahoy there!"

"Even the mysterious voice seems stronger here," Al observed, scanning the empty paths. "It sounds so close. I wonder who it is?"

"We will soon find out Al, when God decides it's time for us to know," Sam said softly. "Look, that bench under the oak. Perfect spot to enjoy His creations." He paused for a moment. "Don't worry about our mysterious caller. When the time is right, we'll investigate. I suspect it will be someone needing our help."

The ancient oak spread massive limbs above the weathered bench-like protective arms. Before them, a pond lay mirror-still, its surface occasionally broken by waterfowl. Swans moved with silent grace, while Canadian geese performed their morning parade.

"Listen to their songs," Al smiled, settling on the bench. "Even the birds praise Him in their own way."

Morning dog walkers passed with cheerful greetings, their pets' excitement adding joy to the crystalline morning. Each "Good morning!" felt like a small blessing exchanged.

"The café looks inviting," Sam noted, watching steam rise from its chimney into the cold air. "Shall we warm up with tea?"

"Divine suggestion," Al chuckled, rising reluctantly from their peaceful spot. The café's windows glowed with welcome, promising warmth and community. But as they reached for the door, that voice called again:

"Ahoy there!"

"Right on cue," Al said thoughtfully. "Almost like..."

"Like it knows we are listening," Sam finished, his heart flowing with confirmation. "I'm seeing glimpses... a man in need... but not yet. It's not yet quite the right time."

The warmth of the café welcomed them from the chilliness of the winter morning. They had barely settled with their steaming cups when a woman approached, something in her bearing speaking of urgent purpose.

"I hope I'm not intruding," she said hesitantly, "but are you the two fellows from the canal path, the ones staying at Aunty Kalesa's?"

"We are indeed," Sam replied, smiling warmly at the woman. "Please, join us. I'm Sam, and this is Al. Is there something we can help you with?"

"Yes, I've heard of you," she began, her eyes darting between Sam and Al. "I'm Alice. I've seen you going into Aunty's and going to church with her, Coolness, and Marg. I attend the Anglican church just up the road from their church."

Sam offered a warm, encouraging smile. "Well, they are our newfound family, together we are committed to helping people through God's guidance. We're just visiting for a short time. So, Alice, how are you?"

"All things considered, I guess I'm fine," Alice responded. But there was something more, a weight behind her words that demanded attention. Her hands clasped and unclasped nervously. "It's not me I'm worried about," she continued, her voice dropping to an intense whisper. "It's a dear friend of mine, Penny."

Sam leaned forward slightly, his posture radiating attentiveness.

"What's troubling you about Penny?" he asked gently.

Alice's story began to pour out, each word carefully chosen yet laden with emotion. "She's in love with the wrong man. She's fallen for him, hook, line, and sinker. She just refuses to see the truth behind his put-on persona."

Sam's eyes narrowed slightly; his investigative instincts immediately engaged.

"Tell us more," he encouraged.

"His name is Gerald," Alice explained, her frustration palpable. "He's a Vicar without a church, he now takes part in our church. Thirty-five years old, while Penny is 46. He's good-looking, with heaps of charisma. When he preaches, all the ladies are focused on him."

Al exchanged a meaningful glance with Sam. They had seen this pattern before, spiritual leaders who used their position to manipulate.

"But there's more," Alice continued, her voice dropping even lower. "Every week, Penny has a Bible teaching session with a local youth leader, Jenny - she's 25, very attractive. And here's where it gets complicated."

Sam leaned forward; his full attention now captured. "Go on," he prompted.

Alice's frustration bubbled over.

"When Jenny is with Penny, Gerald always comes round and insists on walking Jenny home. It's less than five minutes away, but it takes him two hours each time. When Penny questions him, he just says, *'Oh, we get talking, chatting away. She always makes tea.'*"

"And you believe something more is happening?" Al asked, his tone gentle but probing.

"I know something is happening," Alice responded sharply. "But that's not even the worst part. He's offered to be Penny's financial advocate, to take over all her financial dealings. Penny owns two houses, you see - one she's living in and one she rents out.

Sam knew the verse that spoke of this very same situation, "2 Timothy 2:26 talks about the traps of the devil and to be aware of them. It tells us not to be held captive. I think she's been misguided by the devil, so she will fall into a ditch of shame and misfortune. She is following a blind leader, Gerald," responded Sam, his investigative mind was already working. "What did Penny say about this?"

Alice's imitation of Penny's voice was laden with frustration.

"'She says ... '*Well, he's so helpful. He wants to protect me from the stress of my financial affairs. He really is a thoughtful person. I don't know what I'd do without him.*' Can you believe that reply? To me, she is walking headlong into a trap." A heavy silence fell between them. "Can you help?" Alice finally asked her voice a mixture of hope and desperation. "She needs help to see the truth about this rotter of a man."

The word "help" hung in the air - not just a request, but a prayer. A plea for intervention. Sam and Al exchanged a look, a silent communication born of understanding spiritual manipulation.

"We'll need more details," Al said slowly. "Every piece of information matters."

Sam nodded; his voice filled with compassion. "Tell us everything you know about Gerald, about Penny, and about their relationship. Leave nothing out."

As Alice began to speak, the noise of the busy cafe around them seemed to fade. What mattered now was the truth, and how they might help Penny escape a potentially dangerous situation.

"This Gerald," Al said carefully, his pastoral instincts alert to Alice's distress, "he's using his position as Vicar to manipulate trust?"

Alice's knuckles whitened around her cup. "Exactly! And Penny can't see it. Two hours to walk Jenny home, just terrible!" Tears of frustration brightened her eyes. "And now control over her houses..."

Al leaned forward, his face grave with pastoral concern. "We need to meet them both, separately. See Gerald's true face when Penny isn't there to witness his mask slipping."

"Can you arrange that?" Sam asked, with an urgency in his tone.

"Yes... yes, I think so," Alice's hope visible in her straightening shoulders. "I have your details from Aunty. I'll be in touch."

"God will guide us to helping Penny," Sam assured her. "He will show her the truth through love."

Walking back through the crisp wintery morning, that mysterious voice called again:

"Ahoy there!"

"Whoever it is Sam, their calls are becoming more frequent," Al observed thoughtfully.

"As with my vision of the man…." His words trailed off. Regaining his focus, "God is showing me a very lonely heart Al," he added.

Aunty waited in her sitting room, practically vibrating with curiosity. "How was your walk, dears? The park is so lovely this time of year..."

"Divine appointment," Sam said, settling into his favourite chair. "We have news of another lost soul in need," he began, explaining their meeting with Alice. "A vicar using his position to target a vulnerable widow. Two houses at stake, and a secret relationship with a younger woman..."

"Lord have mercy," Aunty breathed, crossing herself.

"We'll need to balance this with Amari's situation," Sam continued. "But Sunday will show us more there. Meanwhile, the Spirit's showing me these cases are connected."

"And that mysterious voice," Al added, "it's getting clearer each time. Seems as if heaven itself is marking our path."

When Coolness and Marg returned," Aunty told them about Sam and Al's encounter "We'll plan together to help Sam and Al. We have more souls needing light, more divine work ahead," she told them decisively, feeling an urgency to help Alice's friend Penny.

The evening wrapped Aunty's sitting room in golden warmth, as they gathered after dinner, the aroma of Aunty's cooking still lingered in the air.

"This Gerald is like a wolf in shepherd's clothing," Coolness whispered, understanding dawning. "Poor Penny..."

Aunty turned to Sam. "What is your plan, Sam?" She asked, setting down her teacup on the small side table next to her chair.

"Meet them separately," Sam confirmed, the warmth of confirmation flowed through him. "See how Gerald behaves when Penny isn't there."

"And Amari?" Marg pressed. "Sunday's meeting is crucial."

"God will help us juggle both," Sam assured them. "The Spirit's showing me these cases are connected, both women needing to see their worth through His eyes, not through those who would exploit them."

"Then we will need a careful timeline," Coolness said thoughtfully, pulling her notebook from her handbag. "Sunday morning we can speak to Amari first, and invite her to stay for coffee and sandwiches in the hall.

"If she agrees," Marg worried, twisting her cross necklace. "You know how she bolts after service."

"That's why we all need positions," Sam explained, his own cross warm with divine guidance. "Al by the door, Coolness with the invitation ready, you and

Aunty creating a pathway of friendly faces..."

"Like shepherds guiding a frightened lamb," Aunty nodded, her eyes wise with years of ministry experience. "And then Penny?"

"Alice is arranging separate meetings," Al confirmed. "First Penny alone, then Gerald, though he won't know we're meeting both."

"He'll try to charm you," Marg warned, her nurse's insight sharp. "I have no doubt about that, not after hearing everything I have about him."

"The Spirit will reveal his true nature," Sam said quietly. "Just as He did with Joe Horton and Duncan." He paused, his thoughts making the connection. "These cases mirror each other, Amari hiding behind perfectionism, Penny behind blind love."

The North Star blazed through the gathering darkness, blessing their guided strategic planning. Two souls seeking light, two missions merging into one divine purpose.

THE WILL
of God prevails

CHAPTER 9

HEALING HEARTS

Morning light painted rainbow patterns through stained glass as the five friends settled into their usual pews near the front of the Church. Sam's heart felt warm with divine purpose as Aunty Kalisa nudged him gently.

"Look," she whispered, smiling, she nodded towards the opposite pews. "This is God's timing, Amari and Alice sitting together."

The two women made a striking pair, Amari elegant in purple Ankara, Alice in her Sunday best. They exchanged warm smiles with the group, though Sam noticed Amari's hands still twisted nervously in her lap.

Sam sensed God guiding him, he stood up and crossed the aisle before the service began. "Wonderful to see you both," he said softly, touching his bible in his hand. "We'll catch up properly after, yes?"

"Looking forward to it," Alice replied warmly, while Amari managed a slight nod.

Pastor Bill's sermon seemed heaven-sent, his words about mental health and social justice flowing from Jeremiah's promise: "For I know the plans I have for you..." The congregation leaned forward as he wove in Paul's assurance that God gives us power, love, and self-discipline, not fear.

"Speaking straight to Amari's heart," Al whispered to Sam, noting how she had stopped fidgeting during certain passages.

The minor hall buzzed with after-service fellowship, steam rising from tea urns like prayers while the conversation flowed. Sam felt divine guidance strengthen as they approached Amari and Alice.

"Amari. Sweet sister," he said gently, "tell us about work. How are things with Jean? We've all been praying..."

The hall grew hushed as Amari spoke, her voice gaining strength with each word. Sunlight through stained glass painted her face in rainbow colours as she described how things had suddenly changed for her.

"I just kept smiling, just like you asked me to," she said softly, her hands steady now, her tone less anxious. "Every time I saw Jeasn, I'd smile, offer her greeting, and thank her. Even when she wouldn't respond..." Her eyes grew distant with memory. "Something inside kept saying 'persist. For a while, she didn't acknowledge me, but I continued to be friendly. On one occasion when I smiled and thanked her for the help and support, she has given me. She sort of half-smiled back at me. That encouraged me.

Sam smiled, nodding his head, confirmation God's healing was at play here. He knew God would keep her strong. Beside him, Coolness wiped happy tears while Marg gripped her sister's hand.

"Then Thursday of last week, Jean and I were included in a work meeting, like a fishbone meeting," Amari continued, animation replacing her usual careful control. "When Jean proposed her ideas... the Spirit just nudged me to support her." Her face glowed with the memory. "That first tiny smile she gave me. like a sunrise after the longest night. Then the manager wanted us to appoint a group leader. I proposed Jean straight away and the group accepted my proposal. Jean was very happy."

"God's timing," Al murmured, pastoral satisfaction evident in his voice.

"But the coffee machine..." Amari's voice caught with emotion. "That's where everything changed. Jean just opened her heart to me, all her fears about being overtaken, being the '*nearly person*.'" She dabbed at her eyes with a delicate handkerchief. "It was so sad, listening to how she has been feeling. She saw me as a threat. Someone who would get a promotion before her. She labelled herself the 'nearly person' because she has been left behind at work so many times. She called me a 'friend, and aplogised for being mean to me.'"

"Oh, Amari!" Coolness sprang forward to embrace her , tears flowing freely now. "Do you see what God has done through your faithfulness?"

Amari's usual perfect composure cracked completely as she returned the hug. "I never thought... never dreamed it could end this way," she whispered, her own tears falling. "When you first suggested smiling at her, Sam, I thought it was impossible."

"Nothing is impossible with God," Sam said softly, reaching out to squeeze Amari's hand. His wise eyes sparkled with joy. "And now look, two hearts healed instead of one!"

"'Love your enemies,'" Al quoted softly. "'Do good to those who persecute you.' You lived it, Amari."

"The Spirit showed me something just now," Sam began, his heart flowing with divine insight. "Remember how we prayed not just for your situation, but for Jean herself? God knew her deeper wounds..."

"The 'nearly person,'" Marg nodded her nurse's heart understanding. "All those times being passed over, letting bitterness take root..."

"Until love wore it away," Sam added, satisfaction rich in his voice. "Patient, persistent, Christ-like love."

Alice, who had been quietly observing, suddenly straightened. "This is exactly what Penny needs to hear," she said urgently. "About love that sees truth instead of just what we want to see..."

"God's perfect timing again," Sam agreed, divine confirmation strong. "Amari, if Jean isn't a Christian, given the right time, you could tell her you are a believer, and that's how God works through people, like the issues you have both been through. She may be open for you to share the Gospel.

"I..." Amari hesitated, old perfectionism warring with new freedom. "I'm not use to speaking about personal things; especially not about God..."

"But that's exactly why others need to hear," Sam pressed gently. "About letting God's love work through our doubts..."

The North Star pulsed visible even through the late morning light, blessing this victory of patient love over fear. One soul restored... and another healing in the process.

After the gathering, the mid-afternoon sunshine blessed their walk home, frost sparkling beneath their feet while the crisp cool air wrapped around them. Joy from Amari's breakthrough still warmed their hearts when that mysterious voice rang out clear as bells:

"Ahoy there!"

"It's getting closure Sam, sounds like it is right here," Al observed, scanning the empty street. "Almost like it's walking beside us."

Sam touched Al's shoulder gently, his tone soft. "The Spirit will reveal all in His time. For now, we have other missions..."

Aunty's house welcomed them with warmth and the promise of a Sunday feast. The rich aromas of roasting chicken drifted from her kitchen, making their mouths water.

"Half an hour till dinner," she announced proud satisfaction in her voice. "I had most of it all ready before we went to Church, fresh chicken, herb potatoes, garden salad..."

"We'll help!" Coolness and Marg chorused, already moving with practiced efficiency. Years of sharing Aunty's kitchen had taught them their roles, with Coolness setting a perfectly arranged table while Marg assisted with final preparations.

The dining room soon filled with the sounds and scents of Sunday blessing. Aunty's best china gleamed in the winter sunlight while steam rose from perfectly roasted chicken like prayers of thanksgiving.

"Aunty," Sam said warmly, savouring each bite, "you've outdone yourself again."

"Pure heaven," Al agreed, reaching for seconds.

Coolness and Marg exchanged knowing smiles. They'd grown up on Aunty's cooking, and watched it comfort countless souls over the years. Every meal was more than food, it was love made tangible; grace served on a plate.

The evening wrapped Aunty's sitting room in golden comfort, the satisfaction of her perfect roast dinner settling over them like a prayer shawl. Flames danced in the fireplace while outside, the North Star emerged early, blessing their rest.

"I don't know how you do it, Aunty," Coolness sighed contentedly from her favourite armchair. "Every Sunday roast is better than the last."

"Practice," Aunty smiled, adjusting the chair with practiced grace. "And love. Food tastes better when it's cooked with prayer."

"Speaking of prayer," Marg said softly, "I can't stop thinking about Penny. After seeing Amari's breakthrough today..."

"God is at work here with divine healing," Sam explained. "I keep seeing connections between their situations."

Al nodded thoughtfully, pastoral insight clear in his expression. "Both are trapped by fear in different ways. Amari behind perfectionism, Penny behind blind love..."

"But love broke through Jean's defences," Coolness reminded them. "Maybe that's the key with Gerald too?"

"Not the same kind of love," Aunty said wisely, pouring more tea into her best cups. "Sometimes love means facing hard truths."

"I just pray Alice can arrange those meetings soon," Sam said quietly. "Before Gerald gets his hands on those house deeds... The Spirit's showing me something, How Jean's confession about being the 'nearly person' opened the way for healing..."

"You think Gerald has similar wounds?" Marg asked, leaning forward.

"Or using others' wounds to hide his own," Sam replied. "Either way, God will reveal the truth in His time."

Suddenly, the evening peace shattered as Sam's phone rang, its chime seeming to echo divine purpose. Seeing, Alice's name pop up on the display, he couldn't hide his gratitude as he answered.

Alice's had urgent with news, "Sam? It's happening, Penny's agreed to meet!" The excitement in Alice's voice was palpable. "Could you and Al come tomorrow evening at six?"

"For God's work we will always be ready," Sam replied, feeling the warmth of divine confirmation strengthen. "We'll be there."

"Let me pick you up," Alice offered quickly. "Five forty-five? I know where Aunty Kalisa's is..."

"That would be wonderful," Sam agreed, catching Al's questioning look. "We'll be waiting."

"Bless you both," Alice's voice carried profound relief. "See you then."

Sam turned to the others, who waited with barely contained anticipation.

"Tomorrow evening," he announced, his cross pulsing warm in his fingers. "Alice is picking us up at five forty-five."

"Thank the Lord," Aunty breathed, exhailing a sigh of relief. "The first step toward helping dear Penny."

"Just like with Amari," Coolness observed thoughtfully. "God opening doors at exactly the right moment."

The North Star blazed brightly through gathering darkness, blessing this next phase of their mission. Another soul seeking light, another divine healing about to unfold.

Penny's Victorian cottage stood as a testament to careful preservation and quiet elegance. Nestled along a gentle street lined with aged oak trees, the cottage glowed with welcome against the gathering dusk. Soft amber light spilt from mullioned windows, casting a warm invitation against the deepening twilight.

The exterior spoke of careful maintenance, soft cream-coloured walls with delicate sage-green trim around the windows and door. Climbing winter rose buds, traced their way up a trellis beside the entrance, their fading summer blooms a gentle reminder of passing time.

Penny opened the door before they could knock, her smile bright but brittle with barely hidden anxiety.

"Welcome, welcome!" Her hands fluttered nervously as she ushered them inside. "Alice has told me so much about you both."

Stepping inside was like entering a carefully curated memory. The hallway revealed polished hardwood floors, their rich patina speaking of decades of loving care. An antique hall stand, a beautiful piece with intricately carved wood and a small mirror held a collection of carefully arranged family photographs and a delicate china dish for keys.

Taking their coats, Penny hung them up neatly on a wooden coat stand. She ushered her guests into the sitting room.

"Do sit down, please. Please make yourself comfortable. I will go and make us all some tea." She turned to Alice. "Alice, it really is nice seeing you again. Would you help me with the tea?

Alice leaned in for a hug. "Lovely to see you again too Penny, of course, I'd be happy to help." The two friends chattered together happily as they pottered around the kitchen. Moments later, they reappeared with a tray, loaded with tea, biscuits and four slices of sponge cake on separate plates.

The living room was a picture of comfortable 18th century charm. A deep burgundy Chesterfield sofa, its leather softened by years of use, sat opposite a fireplace with an elegant carved wooden mantel. Vintage lace curtains filtered the evening light, creating a soft, almost ethereal atmosphere.

Handmade cushions in complementary shades of cream, burgundy, and sage adorned the sofa and an accompanying armchair. A beautiful hand-knitted throw, likely created by Penny herself or a loved one, was draped carefully over the sofa's arm.

On the side table, a collection of items told a story, a silver-framed photograph of what appeared to be ageing parents, a small crystal vase with fresh-cut flowers, and a well-worn Bible with a leather bookmark peeking out. A pair of reading glasses sat neatly beside a coaster, suggesting a life of quiet prayer and contemplation. The room whispered of a woman of depth, cultivated, spiritual, but slightly lonely. Every item seemed carefully chosen and meticulously placed. The space was immaculately clean, but there was a subtle sense of waiting, as if the cottage held its breath, anticipating something.

Sam sensed God speaking to him as he sat observing Jenny exchange pleasantries with Alice. It was clear the two friends were close to each other, their smiles, exchanging knowing looks, as they spoke of past memories and the escaped laughter in their retelling. He sensed Penny's jovial, carefree disposition. She had such a warm trusting soul and it pained him, knowing he was about to be the bearer of news she wouldn't want to hear.

"How's Gerald?" he asked carefully, watching her face.

Penny's expression transformed at his name, love and uncertainty warring in her eyes. "He's wonderful, so thoughtful..." Her hands twisted in her lap. "He wants to help me, you see. Says I'm... stressed. That I have mental issues..."

Al and Alice exchanged alarmed glances as Penny repeated Gerald's words about power of attorney. Sam felt divine guidance strengthen with each of her revelations.

"Dear heart," he said finally, leaning forward with careful gentleness. "We need to speak truth in love right now. Gerald isn't trying to help you. I'm afraid he's systematically undermining your confidence to gain control of your assets."

Penny's face paled. "But he loves me..."

"While spending two hours walking Jenny home," Alice said softly, taking her friend's hand. "Think about it Penny."

"There is nothing wrong with your mind," Sam continued. "But there is everything wrong with someone using false love to steal your future. We speak to you in the name of Jesus Penny. God is giving us confirmation that you need protection, not control."

Tears filled Penny's eyes as truth began to penetrate love's blind wall. "What... what should I do?"

"First, get a mental health assessment," Sam said firmly. "Prove Gerald's lies for what they are. Then we'll confront Jenny, she may be another victim or part of his scheme."

The room felt charged with a mixture of pain, anger, and emerging strength. Penny's hands trembled slightly as she spoke, her voice a complex mixture of vulnerability and growing resolve.

"I don't want to admit the truth," she began, her words catching slightly. "But I can't ignore it any longer."

Sam leaned forward, his posture both supportive and attentive. "Take your time, Penny," he encouraged softly. "We're here to listen."

Her tone was edged with self-blame. "I don't want to but in truth, I believe Gerald is in a relationship with Jenny. One of my friends, Margaret from the church, she saw them together. Holding hands, can you believe it?" The last words came out as a whisper, a private pain finally being acknowledge and made public.

Al's response was gentle. "Discovering betrayal is never easy," he said. "Especially when it involves someone you trusted completely."

Penny's eyes blazed suddenly. "I want to face this issue head-on. My relationship with Gerald has turned completely sour. I see him now, truly see him, for the con man he is." Her voice grew stronger with each word like a river breaking through a dam. "I was completely fooled," she continued, a mixture of anger and self-reflection colouring her tone. "He was so charismatic, so good-looking. Those promises he made - they were like a spell. Beautiful words that meant absolutely nothing."

Sam nodded, encouraging her to continue. "Recognizing the manipulation is the first step to breaking free," he said.

"I'm ready to stand up to him," Penny declared, her voice suddenly firm. "No more hiding, no more pretending. But I'm worried about Jenny. Is she just another victim? Or is she a willing participant in his... whatever this is?" Her final words carried a note of genuine concern. "I just hope Jenny isn't part of his plan to swindle me. My properties, my finances," her voice trialed off.

The room fell silent. The weight of her confession hung in the air, a moment of profound personal reckoning.

Sam spoke softly, "You're not alone in this, Penny. We're here to help you navigate whatever comes next."

Penny looked up, and for the first time, a glimmer of hope replaced the fear in her eyes. The process of reclaiming her life had begun.

Sam leaned forward; his voice gentle but direct. "Do you want backup when you tell Gerald it's over?" The question hung in the air, laden with unspoken support.

Penny's tone was sharp, edged with newfound strength. "Backup? No. I want to take him on all fronts. Alone." Her fingers drummed against the armchair, a rhythm of determination.

Al exchanged a quick glance with Sam. "We can still speak with Jenny," he offered. "Make sure she understands the full picture."

"Absolutely," Penny replied, her voice cutting through the room. "If you could have a word with Jenny and see how far she is involved with this scoundrel."

"No worries, we'll speak to Jenny about Gerald's manipulations." added Sam. "Find out exactly what is going on with them. If she is in on a scam with him, God will reveal the truth about them." His words were a promise, not a suggestion.

Alice watched her own determination a palpable force in the room. "I want to be part of this," she interjected. "But strategically. Sam and Al can handle Jenny. I will just go with them to observe what happens."

The energy shifted. What had begun as a conversation of vulnerability was transforming into a strategic operation of reclaiming power.

As Sam, Al, and Alice prepared to leave, Penny's vulnerability surfaced briefly. "Thank you," she whispered, her voice catching. "All of you, you've given me something precious."

Alice was instantly at her side, hand squeezing Penny's. "We've given you what was always yours," she said firmly. "Your strength. Your voice."

Penny's laugh was watery but genuine. "Some knight in shining armour you are," she teased Alice.

"More like a lioness," Alice shot back. "And don't you forget it."

Their laughter filled the room, a sound of healing, of friendship stronger than any manipulation. Sam and Al watched, understanding the love passing between them. This was more than an intervention. This was a rescue.

As they stepped out, the evening air felt charged with possibility. Gerald had no idea what was coming. The North Star blazed through the darkness; blessing truth spoken with love. Another soul beginning to see light through deception's shadows.

The warm glow of Auntie's living room seemed to pulse with anticipation. Coolness and Marg leaned forward, their eyes locked on Sam and Al, while Auntie hovered nearby, her hands clasped with maternal intensity.

"Well?" Auntie prompted, her voice a mixture of concern and excitement. "How did your meeting with Penny go?"

Al's laugh was short, sharp, a sound of triumph barely contained. "Productive doesn't begin to cover it," he said, exchanging a meaningful glance with Sam. "Penny's had her eyes opened. Completely."

Sam nodded, picking up the thread. "Gerald's days of manipulation are numbered. Penny's transformation was... remarkable." His voice carried a note of respect, of admiration for Penny's emerging strength.

"She's ready for a showdown," Al continued, his excitement building. "And when I say ready, I mean ready. Gerald won't know what hit him." He mimicked a boxing motion, his eyes sparkling with a combination of humour and strategic intent.

Coolness leaned forward. "Tell us everything," she urged.

The story spilled out, Penny's gradual awakening, her new determination to confront Gerald, the intricate web of manipulation they'd uncovered. Sam and Al painted a picture of a woman reclaiming her power, piece by piece.

"We're planning to meet with Jenny next," Sam explained. "Get a full picture of her involvement. Alice is coordinating everything."

Marg's voice was soft but sharp. "Be careful," she warned. "These situations can be unpredictable."

"Always," Sam assured her. His words carried the weight of countless previous interventions and the Divine protection of God.

Auntie bustled to the kitchen. "Tea," she announced. "Every good strategy needs tea." The room erupted in laughter, a moment of lightness in the midst of serious planning

After they had finished their refreshments, Al stretched, the day's tension finally releasing. "My body clock's telling me it's time to rest," he said. "Tomorrow could be a long day."

"Shall we turn in and see what the morning brings?" Sam asked his rhetorical question hanging in the air like a promise.

As they prepared for bed, the house seemed to settle around them. Another chapter was about to unfold, another moment of truth approaching.

The morning light spilled across Auntie's kitchen, bathing the room in a golden glow. Sam's mobile chirped to life, shattering the comfortable morning chatter.

Alice's voice crackled through the phone, electric with expectancy. "I've got it all set up," she announced, her words tumbling out with barely contained energy. "Jenny meeting us. 6:30 pm. At my place."

Sam's eyebrow raised, a subtle signal of intrigue. "What about Penny seeing

Gerald?" he asked, knowing Alice was already three steps ahead.

"It's all perfectly synchronized," Alice replied. "Penny's confronting Gerald at the exact same time. It's like a choreographed dance of justice."

Marg leaned forward; her hands wrapped around a steaming mug of tea. "A dance of justice," she repeated softly, a hint of both admiration and concern in her voice.

"I'll pick you both up," Alice continued. "I want to make sure everything goes smoothly."

As Sam ended the call, the room seemed to collectively exhale. Coolness leaned back, a sardonic smile playing at the edges of his mouth.

"Justice will soon be done," she proclaimed, his voice a mixture of satisfaction and righteous anticipation. "The rotter will get his comeuppance."

"It's not about vengeance," Al cautioned. "It's about truth. About protection."

Auntie moved about the kitchen, her movements a comforting rhythm. "The Lord works in mysterious ways," she murmured, part prayer, part observation.

Sam watched the group in silence, feeling the weight of their collective purpose. These moments before the confrontation, before the truth are revealed, were always the most charged. Anticipation hung in the air like electricity before a storm.

"We'll need to be careful," he said finally. "Cornered people can be unpredictable."

Coolness's laugh was sharp. "Gerald's been unpredictable enough. Time he faced some consequences."

As morning light continued to fill the room, they began to prepare. Meetings would be held. Truths would be spoken. And Gerald's web of manipulation would finally begin to unravel.

Alice's living room was a picture of comfort, a space that spoke of decades of life lived with intention. Soft blue-green walls were adorned with watercolour landscapes and family photographs, each frame telling a silent story. An antique Persian rug, its colours muted by years of gentle use, covered rich hardwood floors. Two well-worn leather armchairs faced a vintage sofa, creating an intimate conversation space that seemed to invite confidences. The soft evening light filtered through delicate lace curtains, casting shadows that danced with the weight of unspoken truths. A small side table held a crystal vase with fresh lavender, its subtle fragrance a counterpoint to the tension in the room.

Sam's fingers drummed an anxious rhythm against the armrest of the leather chair, the soft leather creaking beneath his touch. His eyes, usually calm, held a mixture of determination and concern.

"I hope she comes," he murmured, his voice barely above a whisper. "There's so much at stake tonight."

Al shifted slightly, his body tense. "Prayer first," he suggested, his hand instinctively reaching out to touch Sam's arm, a gesture of solidarity and spiritual preparation. "God will calm our wait." They bowed their heads, Alice joining them. The prayer was a collective breath, words spoken softly, each syllable a plea for guidance, for protection, for truth. The doorbell's chime shattered the moment like a crystal breaking, sharp, unexpected, and revealing. Alice moved with the grace of someone who has navigated difficult conversations before. Her steps were deliberate, her posture a blend of compassion and strength. As she opened the door, the evening air rushed in, carrying with it a sense of anticipation.

Jenny stood on the threshold, a young woman caught between vulnerability and defensiveness. Her eyes darted between the faces in the room, reading, assessing, wondering. Why had she been invited here? She didn't really know Alice that well.

"Come in," Alice said, her voice a carefully crafted instrument of warmth and authority.

Jenny's entrance was a study in hesitation. Her shoulders were slightly hunched, hands clasped tightly, steps tentative. Sam and Al offered smiles designed to disarm, to create a space of safety.

"Lovely to meet you," Sam said, the words carrying the weight of everything unsaid.

For a moment, the room held silence. "What's this meeting about?" Jenny asked, her voice a mixture of curiosity and growing apprehension.

Sam leaned forward, his approach perfect in compassionate confrontation. "It's about Gerald," he began, each word carefully chosen. "About the web of manipulation, he's been weaving."

The revelations came like a series of precise thunderbolts, Gerald's relationship with Penny, his plans for marriage, the financial control, the psychological manipulation. Each detail was a scalpel, carefully dissecting the layers of deception.

Jenny's face changed through a symphony of emotions, shock, betrayal, and self-recrimination.

"I didn't know," she whispered, her voice breaking like delicate glass. Tears threatened to spill from her eyes from her internal storm.

Al's response was gentle, a balm to her raw emotions. "He was using you," he explained, his voice soft but clear. "Manipulating both you and Penny. Playing a dangerous game of emotional chess."

"I feel like I've betrayed Penny," Jenny lamented, a single tear trailing down her cheek. The weight of her words hung in the air, a confession, a plea for understanding.

Sam's reassurance was immediate, his voice a mixture of compassion and strength. "Penny is confronting him as we speak. She's strong. She sees through his schemes now."

As the conversation continued, a careful deconstruction of Gerald's manipulative tactics. Jenny's defensive walls began to crumble, replaced by a determination to support Penny. "I'll do anything to help her," Jenny declared, her voice finding a newfound resolve.

An hour later, the meeting drew to a close, Sam's final words were both a promise and a shield of protection.

"We're here," he told Jenny, each word a lifeline. "Whatever happens, you're not alone in this."

The room seemed to exhale a collective release of tension, of truth spoken, of a web of manipulation beginning to unravel. Outside, the evening settled, quiet, expectant, waiting.

The sitting room bathed in the glimmering sparkle of the North Star filtered through lace curtains. Sam's entrance brought a wave of weary determination, while Al moved with the unhurried grace of a seasoned investigator.

Marg leaned forward; her hands clasped tightly in her lap. The lines around her eyes spoke of years of compassionate listening. "Tell us everything," she urged her voice balanced between concern and hope

Sam sank into the armchair, its familiar contours embracing him like an old friend. His fingers traced absent patterns on the armrest. "Jenny's more victim than accomplice," he began, each word carefully chosen.

Al nodded his thoughts reflecting on their meeting with Jenny. "It's more complicated than we initially thought," he added, his voice low and reflective.

Coolness, silent until then, spoke up. "So just how deep does this Gerald's manipulation go?"

Sam's tone was short, hard. "Deep enough to break hearts. Deep enough to shatter trust." He paused, collecting his thoughts. "Jenny truly believed she was special. That Gerald genuinely cared."

"The most insidious manipulators are masters of creating that illusion," Aunty interjected, her voice carrying wisdom of decades of observing human nature.

Al glanced around the room; his eyes distant. "It's not just about Gerald," he mused. "It's about the systems that allow such manipulation to flourish. The spiritual blind spots we all carry."

Marg's response was soft but sharp. "How then can we prevent this from happening again?"

"Awareness," Sam said firmly. "Constant, vigilant awareness. Teaching people to recognize the signs. To trust their intuition."

Coolness shifted in her seat. "But it's not always that simple," she challenged. "Love can blind even the most discerning person."

Aunty's tone was knowing, reflecting understanding. "Love doesn't blind," she corrected gently. "Fear does. Fear of being alone. Fear of not being enough."

The room fell silent, the truth of her words hanging in the air like a fragile cobweb.

Al's voice broke the moment. "Jenny's ready to support Penny," he said. "That's something. One victim reaching out to another. There's hope in that."

Aunty shook her head, her tone stern but with a hint of sadness. "We'll wait until morning now," she declared. "There is no point in revealing what you've discovered tonight to Penny now. There is a lot going on in her life at the moment and I'm sure her confrontation with Gerald has left her emotionally drained. Let the dust settle. Give Penny time to breathe, to process the truth. Alice can contact her tomorrow to arrange another visit."

As evening settled around the house, the conversations continued, some spoken, some silent, all profound.

The morning light filtered through Auntie's kitchen window, casting a golden glow pulsating with the warmth of God's protection. Sam's mobile vibrated, breaking the comfortable morning silence.

"Penny's ready," Alice announced, her tone reflective of the events that had revealed themselves.

Sam's body language shifted from relaxed to alert. "Seven this evening?" he confirmed, a subtle seriousness threading through his voice.

Al watched from across the room, his experienced eyes reading the nuances of the conversation. The slight lift of Sam's eyebrow, the way his fingers tightened almost imperceptibly around the phone, were the tells of a man preparing for a significant moment.

"Alice will pick us up," Sam reported to Al and Aunty, his tone a mixture of professional detachment and underlying anticipation.

"I'll inform Coolness and Marg when they return from work," Aunty offered, already mentally organizing the evening's potential outcomes.

"Brilliant!" Sam exclaimed, his mood lifting, his tone changing. "Wherever we go, there's always a team of Christians willing to help, willing to go the extra mile." The room seemed to breathe with their shared sense of gratitude. "God is good all the time," Sam added, it never failed to amaze him how wonderful God's love truly is. How He brought people together to do His work.

Aunty stood up, collecting the teapot from the table. "I'll make us another pot of tea." Opening the fridge, she realised there was no milk left. "Oh dear," she muttered. "It seems we are out of milk.

"No worries, Aunty," Al exclaimed. "Sam and I will walk down to the local shop to get some. Is there anything else you need?"

"Oh! Now that you ask," she laughed, reflecting on what Coolness and Marg always say about her. "Never ask Aunty if she needs anything from the shop. Not unless you have six pairs of hands to carry the load.'

The local shop trip became an unexpected moment of spiritual intrigue. As

Sam and Al walked, the quiet street suddenly erupted with an inexplicable declaration.

"Ahoy there! I be a blagger!"

Al laughed, "There it goes again," he paused, "You know Sam, this may sound daft but it actually sounds like a pirate."

Sam smiled, his eyes twinkled with a knowing sparkle. "It does indeed Al. It does indeed."

Back at Auntie's, Sam and Al put away the groceries put away, a simple task becoming a moment of shared purpose.

"Thanks, guys," said Aunty, three words spoken in appreciation. "I'll make us that fresh pot of tea now."

"Wonderful," chorused Sam and Al in union.

Sitting at the kitchen table, waiting for the kettle to boil. Sam and Al couldn't help but smile as they reflected on their simple walk to the shop. The voice of the mysterious "blagger" hung in the air between them, another thread in their ongoing spiritual tapestry, waiting to be understood.

The evening light filtered through Penny's living room curtains, casting long shadows that seemed to mirror the weight of the recent events. Penny stood by the window, her hands trembling slightly as she arranged a tea tray with a precision that betrayed her inner turmoil. The sound of the kettle's whistle broke the tense silence as Alice, Sam, and Al arrived, their faces etched with a mixture of concern and anticipation.

"Come in," Penny's voice cracked, "Please, sit down."

Sam was the first to notice her fragility. He guided her gently to the armchair, his hand a reassuring touch on her shoulder. "Take your time, Penny," he said softly, his eyes scanning her face with genuine compassion.

Al positioned himself near the window, his posture alert, and protective. Alice sat closest to Penny, her friendship a steady anchor in the stiring emotional storm.

Penny took a deep breath, her fingers tracing the delicate china teacup. "I confronted Gerald," she began, the words tumbling out like shards of broken glass. "Everything we suspected, everything you helped me see, it was all true." Her gaze hardened, a newfound strength replacing the vulnerability that had defined her interactions with Gerald. "He came here thinking he could charm his way out, with that same manipulative smile. But not this time." A bitter laugh escaped her lips. "I exposed every single one of his lies."

Sam leaned forward; his tone gentle with compassion.

"Tell us everything."

"He tried to gaslight me," Penny continued, her voice gaining momentum. "Tried to make me believe I was imagining his financial manipulations, that my perception of his deceit was some kind of mental delusion. But I wasn't going to let him break me down again."

Alice reached out, squeezing Penny's hand.

"You're stronger than he ever gave you credit for."

"When I laid out the evidence," Penny said, her eyes flashing with a mix of hurt and triumph, "his face changed. Gone was the smooth-talking charmer. He was exposed, a fraud stripped bare. Tell me what did Jenny say."

Sam took up the narrative. "Jenny was devastated but more by the betrayal than anything else. She had no idea how deeply Gerald had manipulated both of you. It was like watching someone realize they'd been living next to a stranger all along."

"He used her," Penny said, her voice low. "Turned her into a weapon against me without her even knowing. But not anymore."

Alice's tone was reassuring but firm. "You've reclaimed your narrative, Penny. And we're here, all of us to ensure he can't touch you again."

The room fell into a momentary silence, charged with a complex blend of emotions: relief, anger, solidarity, and healing.

"To new beginnings," Sam finally said, raising an imaginary toast.

Penny looked around at her friends, and for the first time in months, she smiled. A real smile reached her eyes, banishing the shadows of Gerald's manipulation. "To new beginnings," she echoed, her voice steady and strong.

Outside, the North Star gleamed brightly, a visual metaphor for Penny's journey from darkness into light.

The warmth of Aunty's living room enveloped Al and Sam as they entered, their earlier tension melting into welcoming relief. Marg was seated in her favourite armchair, a well-worn knitting project draped across her lap, while Aunty occupied the corner settee. Coolness stood by the window; her silhouette outlined by the soft evening light streaming in.

Aunty's keen eyes swept over the two men, reading the story written in their relaxed postures and victorious expressions. "Judging by those warm smiles on both of your faces," she said, her voice a mix of curiosity and understanding, "it seems like you had a highly successful meeting with Penny."

Al leaned against the mantelpiece, a subtle smile playing on his lips while Sam settled into an armchair, his body language speaking of hard-won peace. "It went better than we could have hoped," Sam began, his voice filled with a mixture of pride and relief.

"Penny was incredible," Al interjected, his respect for her evident. "She didn't just confront Gerald, she completely dismantled him."

Sam nodded, leaning forward with animated enthusiasm. "Every single one of his manipulative plans, the financial schemes, the psychological pressure, she saw through them all. She reduced him to nothing. Left him stammering, trying to apologize, he was completely exposed for the con man he is."

Aunty let out a sigh of relief, her weathered hands clasped together. "It takes tremendous courage to stand up to someone who's been manipulating you," she said softly, a wealth of understanding in her words.

Marg paused her knitting, her needles stilling as she listened intently."These predators think they can break people," she muttered, a rare edge of anger in her usually gentle voice. "But they don't understand the strength of true friendship."

"I don't think he'll dare show his face again," Sam remarked, his tone decisive. "He knows he's been completely exposed. Penny made it clear she won't tolerate his games."

Al chuckled, a sound of genuine amusement. "Game over," he said simply. "Victory to Penny."

The room fell into a companionable silence, the weight of their shared triumph hanging in the air. God had protected both Penny and Jenny, dismantled a manipulator, and restored their friendship. Aunty stood up; she moved towards the kitchen. "Who wants tea?" she called over her shoulder, a note of celebration in her voice.

"I do!" came the collective response, punctuated by warm laughter that seemed to wash away the last remnants of Gerald's dark influence.

The morning light filtered through the kitchen curtains, casting a soft glow on the faces of the gathered friends. Breakfast dishes were still on the table, half-empty coffee mugs telling silent stories of their earlier conversation. Sam leaned forward, his eyes intense with purpose, breaking the comfortable post-breakfast quiet.

"I want to talk about the Pirate," he began, his voice low and serious. The room seemed to collectively hold its breath.

Al raised his eyebrows, "So, you do think it's a Pirate then Sam? You know, I was only joking when I said that."

"Who are we talking about?" quizzed Coolness, intrigue running through her thoughts.

"You know," Al replied. "The mysterious voice that we keep hearing. The one that keeps calling out Ahoy there."

"Arh!" she exclaimed. "So, you think the mysterious voice is the local Pirate then."

Al shook his head, puzzled by her remark. "Are you saying there really is a Pirate living nearby?"

"Of course there is," Aunty declared. "He lives just down the road near the park in that big pirate-themed house."

"How come none of you have mentioned him before now? We've all been hearing that voice for ages, following us and calling out to us."

Aunty shifted in her chair as she caught sight of Sam's amused look. "Well to be honest, I didn't really put the two together. I haven't seen the pirate around for ages. No-one has. I didn't even think he still lived around these parts anymore..." her voice trailed off, as she realised the obvious.

Sam leaned over towards Aunty, placing a comforting hand on her shoulder. "It's alright Aunty, you weren't to know it was him. I wouldn't have known if God hadn't spoken to me about him."

A wave of embarrassment flushed Aunty's cheeks. "Oh, I feel dreadful now. Truth be known, I have never really given him much thought. People around here just write him off as being a crazy ole man. I should have known better. I should have realised he was a soul in need."

Coolness nodded, "Yes, I've heard some very wild stories about him as well.

Al crossed his arms, his brow furrowed in concentration. "He's not some lunatic," he interjected firmly. "This is a person in genuine pain, calling out for help. We can't ignore that."

"And we're not going to Al," Sam said, his tone mirroring his resolve. "Now God has put him in our sights, we will go and find him and see what help he needs."

Marg, who had been quietly listening, finally spoke. Her voice was soft but carried an unmistakable weight of wisdom. "Sometimes people hide in plain sight," she said. "Particularly those carrying the deepest wounds."

"So, you say he lives near the park," Sam questioned repeating Aunty's revelation about a pirate house... "Then that's our starting point." He turned to Al, a glimmer of determination in his eyes. "What do you say? Shall we go investigate?"

Al's lips curled into a slight smile. "Why not? We've solved more complicated mysteries."

"Be careful boys," Aunty warned, her voice was gentle but carried a note of caution. "Someone who's been hiding for so long might not want to be found."

Coolness stood up, moving to a drawer. She pulled out a small notebook and a pencil. "I'll jot down what we know about him," she said. "Every detail might matter." Writing a few details down she passed the notebook to Sam. "There you are Sam, I think thats about everything."

Al stood, stretching. "Ready, Sam?" he asked.

Sam nodded, already moving towards the door. He slipped the notebook into his pocket. "Let's go find our Pirate."

As they prepared to leave, the room was charged with a sense of purpose. This wasn't just a search, it was a mission of compassion, of reaching out to someone who had been calling for help for far too long.

"Keep your phones on," Marg called after them. "We want to know what you find."

The door closed behind Sam and Al, leaving behind a room full of hope, anticipation, and the collective strength of trust in God's love.

The street stretched before Sam and Al like a promise of discovery, lined with modest houses that blended into one another. But as they walked, something extraordinary began to take shape before their eyes.

"Al," Sam breathed, stopping mid-stride, "look at that garden."

It wasn't just a garden. It was a maritime marvel transplanted onto solid ground. A wooden structure, so meticulously crafted that it appeared to be a full-sized galleon frozen in mid-voyage. Intricate woodwork mimicked the curves of a sailing ship, with wooden planks that spoke of countless imaginary voyages. Rigging made of carefully woven ropes hung from elaborate masts, some draped with climbing ivy that seemed to embrace the wooden vessel like seaweed. It was a picture of nautical imagination. Rocks carefully placed resembled waves, with low-growing succulents creating the illusion of sea foam. Maritime plants, sea lavender, beach grass, and salt-tolerant shrubs, created a landscape that whispered of distant shores and endless horizons.

"It's remarkable," Al murmured, his eyes taking in every detail. "Someone's poured their entire soul into this place."

Sam nodded, a sense of amazement settling over him. "This isn't just a garden. This is a story, Al. A story of someone who's never stopped dreaming."

They approached the house, their footsteps careful, almost hesitant. The pathway was lined with maritime-themed decorations, old anchors partially buried in the ground, weathered buoys hanging from nearby trees, and small sculptures that looked like they'd been salvaged from long-forgotten shipwrecks. The house itself seemed to emerge from the galleon-garden, its architecture subtly mimicking the curves of a ship. Windows were positioned like portholes, and the exterior had been painted in deep blues and weathered whites that blended seamlessly with the maritime theme. Sam rang the doorbell, two sharp rings that seemed to echo like a ship's signal bell. Silence.

"No one's home," Sam said after a moment, disappointment evident in his voice.

Al pulled out a small notebook. "Let's document what we've seen. This is too incredible to forget."

They decided to go and wait in the nearby park cafe, offering a perfect view of the street. The cafe was nearly empty, just a few patrons scattered at various tables, creating a sense of peaceful intimacy.

"I've never seen anything quite like that garden," Sam said, wrapping his hands around his coffee mug. "It's like someone's entire life story is told through those plants and wooden structures."

Al nodded; his eyes still distant. "Someone who's been calling out 'Ahoy there!' for years, needing help but never asking for it."

The cafe's quiet allowed their thoughts to drift. Outside, the street remained still, the galleon garden a silent sentinel of truths yet to be revealed.

"Shall we take a walk in the park?" Sam suggested, a spark of hope still burning. "Now that we know who we are looking for, maybe we'll catch a glimpse of our mysterious Pirate."

Al smiled, a mixture of determination and curiosity in his eyes. "Let's go."

Standing to leave, the cafe seemed to hold its breath, as if the walls themselves were keeping watch, waiting for the next chapter of this curious tale to unfold. As they walked on the pathway to the boating lake, they made for a park bench. The boating lake stretched before them, a mirror of tranquillity reflecting the late morning sky. Sam and Al settled onto the weathered bench; its wooden slats worn smooth by countless previous vistors.

Al stretched out his legs, his keen eyes scanning the surroundings. "Quite a spot," he murmured, breathing in the crisp air. Joggers traced familiar paths, children played with kites that danced like colourful spirits against the sky, and elderly couples walked hand in hand, their slow pace a testament to years of shared history.

Sam leaned back; his posture relaxed but his mind clearly elsewhere. "That garden," he said after a while, breaking their comfortable silence. "It's a life waiting to be heard Al."

Al nodded, understanding exactly what Sam meant. "Some people write their life stories in words," he observed, "and some write them in gardens, in wood, in the way they shape the world around them."

"It's been half an hour," Al said, checking his watch. "Shall we try the house again?"

Sam's eyes sparkled with eagerness. "Let's do it." When they approached the remarkable house again, its maritime theme even more striking in the mid-morning light; a figure emerged from the pathway, a local resident, by the look of him.

Sam's approach was warm, open, smiling at the stranger. "Hi there," he called out, his voice friendly but purposeful. "Do you know the guy who lives here?"

The fellow studied them for a moment, caution evident in his stance. "Yes, he'll be back later. What do you want with him?" There was something protective in his tone, a hint of wariness that suggested the residents of this street knew their neighbour was unique, but perhaps understod he preferred solitude.

Sam's response was carefully crafted. "Well, let's just say he'll be happy to see us. If he should need any help, Al and I will be here to support him."

The subtle emphasis on 'support' seemed to ease the fellow's tension. His demeanour softened slightly. "He's usually an early riser," he replied. "Any time before 11 am. That's when you'll catch him."

"That's perfect," Sam responded, a gentle smile playing on his lips. "We'll drop by tomorrow at about 10 am. Thanks for the information."

As the fellow walked away, Al turned to Sam.

"Interesting," he murmured. "Someone who knows him but seems both distant and protective."

Sam nodded, his gaze returning to the extraordinary garden. "We're getting closer to understanding, Al. I can feel it."

The tea tray clattered slightly as Aunty set it down, her hands trembling with barely contained curiosity. "Well?" she stated, her white-streaked hair catching the lamplight, eyes boring into Sam and Al. "Don't keep us in suspense!"

Sam smiled, the memory of the pirate's house played in his thoughts. He dropped into an armchair, his shoulders folding in a way that suggested both exhaustion and exhilaration.

"You wouldn't believe it if I told you," he said, reaching for a teacup.

Al leaned forward, his hands wrapped around his mug, knuckles showing the map of years of hard work. "The garden," he began, then paused, searching for words. "It was... more than a garden."

Coolness jumped in, her typically reserved demeanour crackling with an animated spark. "More than a garden? I don't understand What does that even mean?"

"The house," Sam interjected, "it's extraordinary. It has a garden that looks like a galleon, carefully crafted down to the smallest detail. It's like someone's entire life story is told through wood, plants, and maritime memories."

Coolness tilted her head, fascinated. "And the Pirate. Did you find out if he is the one calling out 'Ahoy there' all the time?"

"We haven't met him yet," Al explained. "But we spoke to a neighbour who confirmed he'll be home tomorrow morning. We're planning to visit around 10."

As evening settled, they moved to their nightly ritual of prayer. But this time, the prayer felt different. It was more of a collective breath of hope, and of anticipation.

Aunty's voice trembled slightly as she began. "We come together," she said, "not just as friends, but as witnesses to so many unfinished stories. Lord continue your guidance of Sam and Al as they prepare to do your work. Amen."

"Amen," the other whispered, gratitude, love and beating hearts of acceptance. With hands joined. Eyes closed. The room seemed to vibrate with unspoken possibilities.

"Tomorrow," Sam whispered, so softly only Al could hear, "we bring someone home." ...And in that moment, home felt like the most beautiful word in the world...

I PRAY THAT
you would find
COMFORT
IN THE TRUTH OF
god's word

CHAPTER 10

SOLVING THE MYSERY

The mysterious '*Ahoy there!*' had finally led Sam and Al to a house that seemed to have sailed straight out of the Golden Age of Piracy. As they approached the front door, it suddenly swung open. Standing in the open doorway to greet them was the man they had been searching for.

He was well over six feet tall and a mountain of a man. His thick, salt and pepper grey beard cascaded down to his chest, braided in several places and adorned with small copper rings that caught the morning light. His face was a landscape map of experiences, deep set blue eyes that held the colour of stormy seas, skin weathered like old teak, with lines etched so deeply they seemed to tell stories of their own. He wore a deep blue peacoat that had seen better days, patched in places but meticulously maintained. Underneath, a cream coloured cable-knit sweater hinted at maritime tradition. His trousers were dark canvas, tucked into well-worn leather boots that looked like they'd walked a thousand miles.

"Welcome aboard, lads," he rumbled, voice deep as ocean swells. "I'm the Blagger you've been seeking. I've been expecting you. Enter my galleon home."

Following him into his house, Sam felt his cross in his pocket pulse warm as they stepped into what could only be described as a maritime museum come to life. The living room, a carefully curated shrine to nautical history. Dark wooden floors, the colour of rich mahogany, were partially covered by worn woven nautical rugs. The walls were a deep navy blue, almost black, creating a sense of being inside the hull of an pirate ship. Replica black powder kegs lined one wall; their wooden surfaces were polished to a soft sheen. Cannonballs were arranged in strategic pyramids, each looking like it had been pulled directly from an 18th-century ship's arsenal. A massive binnacle, an old ship's compass housing, stood proudly near a bay window, sunlight catching its brass fittings. There was a skull and crossbones flag in the corner of the room, not just a decoration, but a statement, faded, but still proud, with threads of embroidery that suggested generations of maritime history.

"Magnificent," Al breathed, taking in the Jolly Roger that dominated one corner.

Sam's eyes were wide, his body leaning forward with uninhibited curiosity. "Wow!" he exclaimed, his voice cracking with excitement. "What a remarkable room! Are you really a Blagger?"

The man's weather-beaten face softened.

"More a Bellamy man myself," he admitted, settling into what appeared to be an actual captain's chair. "Truth is, I'm descended from one of the lesser known pirates of the 1700s. Not your Blackbeards or Calico Jacks, mind you, but pirate blood runs true all the same. "I'm Robert Bow," he said, as if the name itself was both a confession and a challenge. "But some call me Rob the Pirate."

"Rob, it is then," said Sam preferring to use his christian name. "I'm Sam and this is my friend Al," He held his hand out in Al's direction as a form of introduction.

Al watched carefully, his experienced eyes taking in every detail. When Rob had mentioned *'he had been expecting them,'* Al had noticed a subtle tension ripple through Rob's body.

"You said you've been expecting us," Al pressed gently, his tone a careful balance of curiosity and respect. "What did you mean?"

Something vulnerable flickered in Rob's ocean blue eyes.

"Aye, that I was. But the telling..." He gestured helplessly at his surroundings. "It's not as ship-shape as it appears, lads. Been taking on water these past few years, if you take my meaning. Truth be told, "I'm going through a difficult time," he admitted, his voice suddenly smaller. "Let's just say things aren't as they used to be." A tremor passed through his large frame, vulnerability fighting with pride

Sam leaned forward, his hand instinctively reaching out, not quite touching, but offering support. "We're here to help," he said softly.

Rob's eyes, flickered with a complexity of emotions. He straightened himself in his chair, hope beginning to replace the haunting in his expression.

"Thing is, I've heard about you two. Heard how you help folk find their way back to safe harbour. And I'm... well, I'm a bit lost at sea myself."

Sam's gaze drifted to the corner of the room, where a dark, mysterious cloak hung draped over a large object. His curiosity burned like a lighthouse beacon, but God had taught him patience.

"That cloak," Sam said softly, his voice a gentle probe, "The one in the corner, I sense it holds special meaning."

Rob's weather-beaten face tightened, his eyes suddenly stormy with emotion.

"Aye, that's the Cloak of Happiness," he said softly, his usual theatrical manner falling away. "What lies beneath..." His voice caught. "That's a tale for another tide if you take my meaning. Some things aren't ready to be revealed. Not yet."

Sam straightened himself up; his posture open but not intrusive. "We're not here to force anything," he said, his words carefully chosen. "We're here to listen, to understand."

Moisture gathered in Rob's eyes. "You understand then? About needing time to find the right words?"

Sam's hand inched toward Rob, not touching, but offering a silent support. "Everyone has their own journey," he said. "And everyone deserves a chance to walk that journey with dignity."

A single tear traced a path down Rob's weathered cheek. He didn't wipe it away, letting it be a testament to his vulnerability. "You're becoming my friends," Rob said, his voice thick with emotion. "Today feels like... like the beginning of something important."

Al's smile was gentle, understanding. "Small steps," he said. "We'll meet again on Friday. No pressure, no expectations. Just friendship."

Rob's laugh was unexpected, a rich, rolling sound that seemed to shake the maritime artefacts around them. "Friday at 6 pm then," he confirmed. "Here in my galleon home."

As Sam and Al prepared to leave, the cloak remained a silent sentinel of the untold stories, and promising revelations yet to come.

Sam paused at the doorway, turning back. "Blessings to you, Rob," he said, and the words felt like a baptism of friendship.

The warmth of Auntie's house enveloped Sam and Al like a welcoming embrace. Soft lamplight created golden pools across the living room, casting gentle shadows on the familiar faces of Aunty, Coolness, and Marg. Their anticipation was obvious, eagerly awaiting news from the boys. Aunty sat in her favourite armchair, her hand-knitted shawl draped around her shoulders, her eyes bright with curiosity.

"Well?" she asked, her voice a mixture of excitement and maternal concern. "Tell us everything! I've been praying non-stop since you left."

Sam dropped into the nearest armchair, his body language telling a story before his words could. He ran a hand through his hair, a gesture of both exhaustion and exhilaration.

"It was..." he paused, searching for the right words, "It's like stepping into a pirate museum..."

"Complete with cannon balls and powder kegs," Al added, his eyes bright with remembered wonder. "And the man himself, Rob the Pirate..."

"A real pirate!" exclaimed Coolness as she leaned forward, "Tell us everything," she urged, her curiosity sparked.

"He's a descendant of pirates," Sam replied, his voice low and reflective. "Not just any pirates, maritime legends from the early 1700s. But there's something more. Something thats hidden."

Marg's hands stilled on her knitting needles. "Hidden?" she asked, her voice soft but sharp.

Sam nodded towards Al, a silent communication passing between them.

"A cloak," he explained. "The 'Cloak of Happiness,' Rob called it. It's covering something he's not ready to reveal."

Aunty's eyes narrowed, wisdom sparkling in their depths. "Sometimes," she said slowly, "our deepest hurts are the things we keep covered the longest."

"Whatever it is," Sam paused, "God has told me it's significant, it's the key to the storm he's weathering."

Coolness stood, moving to put the kettle on. The familiar ritual of tea making seemed to ground them, to create a moment of normality in the midst of their extraordinary discovery.

"We're meeting again on Friday," Al said. "At 6 pm. In his 'galleon home,' as he calls it."

Marg's smile was knowing. "Sounds like this one is a challenge," she said, "but one, you're both perfectly suited for."

Sam laughed, a rich, warm sound that seemed to fill the room. "Rob said we're becoming his friends," he said softly. "That really made my day, knowing he felt we could be his friends."

As night settled around the house, the room was alive with possibility.

"God is good," Aunty murmured, echoing her earlier words. But this time, it felt like a prayer of anticipation, of hope. After bidding each other good night. Sam and Al climbed up the stairs, pleasantly exhausted but filled with divine purpose. The North Star blessed their rest through diamond-paned windows while alone in his pirate house, Rob was about to witness the true healing power of divine love.

After breakfast, Sam and Al made their way to the park. The morning sunshine blessed the park with frost sparkling on bare branches while the North Star faded into morning grey. Wandering familiar paths, their footsteps crunching on frozen grass as they watched early joggers and dog walkers all enjoying God's creation.

"Perfect spot," Al said contentedly as they settled on their favourite bench beneath the ancient oak. His pastoral heart always found peace here, watching God's creatures go about their morning business.

Sam reached inside his pocket, touching his cross, he felt its familiar warmth. "Fancy a coffee now?"

Al's laugh was soft, carefree. "Now that my friend is a good idea," he grinne

The café welcomed them with steam-clouded windows and the rich aroma of fresh brew. They'd barely settled with their cups when a familiar voice called out,

"Sam! Al!" Alice hurried over, joy radiating from her face. "I hoped I'd see you here!"

"Divine appointment," Sam laughed, gesturing to an empty chair. "Tell us, how is everything."

"You first," Alice insisted, her eyes bright with curiosity. "Have you found out any more about the mysterious voice?"

"Yes, we have. It led us to a man called Rob Bow," Sam explained, warming his hands around his cup. "We meet him yesterday, you should see his house Alice, it is something else. Like a maritime museum..."

"And Gerald?" Al asked gently, noting how seemed so joval.

Alice's face transformed with satisfaction."Gone!" she announced triumphantly. "Slipped away in the night when his schemes were exposed. But the real blessing..." Her eyes filled with happy tears. "Penny and Jenny are friends again, supporting each other in healing."

"God's love is the love of healing," Sam said softly, his heart flowing with gratitude. "As Aunty always says, God is good."

"The best part?" Alice stood, gathering her things. "They're both coming to church now, together! I'd love to stay and chat, but I'm meeting a friend from church. A newcomer I've been mentoring."

Her departure was as bright and quick as her arrival. Sam and Al watched her go, the cafe's warmth surrounding them.

"What a pleasurable encounter," Sam mused, taking a sip of his coffee.

Al's laugh was rich, reflective. "God," he said, "always has a way of surprising us."

Walking home through the crystalline morning, Sam felt divine satisfaction settle in his heart. "One mission accomplished," he said quietly. "Another just beginning..." The North Star pulsed once more before fading completely, blessing their journey forward. More souls seeking light, more divine appointments waiting to unfold.

The kitchen at Aunty's house was a sanctuary of warmth and comfort. Aunty moved with grace as she prepared tea, her movements as always, deliberate and purposeful.

Sam and Al entered, carrying the crisp energy of their morning park visit. Their faces were alight with a mixture of joy and anticipation, the look of those who know they're part of something larger than themselves.

Aunty's keen eyes took them in, reading their body language like an open book. "You've got that look," she said, her voice a blend of wisdom and gentle teasing. "The park must have been good to you today."

Sam dropped into a chair, his slender frame relaxing into the familiar space.

"We ran into Alice," he said, a smile playing at the corners of his mouth. "Quite the unexpected encounter."

Aunty passed a mug of tea over to Al. Leaning against the kitchen counter he accepted it with gratitude.

"Penny and Jenny," Sam continued, his voice softening. "They've reconnected. And Gerald?" He paused, a hint of satisfaction in his tone. "That blighter has gone. Completely."

Aunty's response was a knowing smile. Her hands, weathered by years of living and loving, began to knead some bread dough, a physical manifestation of her nurturing spirit.

"Grace works in the most mysterious ways," she murmured.

Al smiled, "Speaking of mysteries," he said, shifting the conversation, "we've got our second meeting with Rob tomorrow."

"The Pirate," Aunty said, her eyes twinkling. It wasn't a question, but an acknowledgement.

Al nodded, his body language speaking volumes. "That cloak he spoke of the 'Cloak of Happiness,' Sam is right, it's more than just a piece of fabric."

Sam leaned forward, his hands gesturing as he spoke.

"We're building a relationship Al," he said. "But I have to admit with Rob, it feels like we're navigating uncharted waters. We can't predict where this journey will lead."

Aunty stopped kneading, her hands resting on the flour-dusted surface. "The best journeys rarely can be predicted," she said softly. "They're about trust. About listening."

"Christian journeys," Sam reflected, his voice low and thoughtful, "are never straight lines. They're more like... elaborate tapestries. Each thread unexpected, but somehow perfectly placed."

Al reached out, squeezing Sam's shoulder, a gesture of solidarity that spoke more than words ever could.

Smling, Aunty returned to her bread, the rhythmic kneading a counterpoint to their conversation. Outside, the day continued, full of promise, full of many possibilities.

The atmosphere in Auntie's living room was charged with a mixture of anticipation and quiet determination. Sam stood by the window, his reflection overlaying the evening landscape, a man balanced between uncertainty and hope.

"I must be honest. I am feeling nervous," he admitted, his voice barely above a whisper. His fingers traced an invisible pattern on the windowpane, betraying the inner turbulence beneath his composed exterior.

Al moved closer, his presence a steady anchor.

"Nervousness and faith aren't opposites," he said softly. "They're companions on the same journey."

Coolness stood near the doorway, her posture radiating quiet strength. Her eyes, deep and perceptive studied Sam and Al with a mixture of maternal concern and unwavering confidence."God doesn't call the qualified," she said, her voice rich with conviction. "He qualifies the called."

Sam turned, a tremulous smile breaking through his anxiety.

"Your words," he said, "they bring me immense comfort Coolness. You do seem to always know exactly what to say."

"I've learnt it from Aunty," she flashed Sam a broad grin.

Marg bustled about, preparing a small care package, flask of tea, some homemade biscuits, practical expressions of her support. "Keys?" she asked, holding them out. "Phone charged?"

Al patted his pocket, a ritual of preparation. "Check and check," he responded.

"We don't know what Rob's 'Cloak of Happiness' conceals," Sam murmured, more to himself than to anyone else. "But when he's ready to tell us, we'll be there for him."

Coolness stepped forward, her hands outstretched. "May I?" she asked, gesturing a spiritual communion. They formed a circle, hands joined. The prayer that followed was not loud, not dramatic, but powerful in its quiet intensity. A prayer of protection, of guidance, and of open hearts.

"Go," Aunty said, hurrying them on, her eyes glistening. "Remember your compassion is your greatest strength."

The evening air embraced them as they walked to Marg's car, two friends, united in God's love, stepping into the unknown.

At Rob's house, Sam's hand hesitated for just a moment before knocking. A heartbeat of anticipation. Of possibility. The door opened. Rob stood before them, the Pirate, the mystery, waiting to be understood.

"Welcome," he greeted, his voice carrying a mixture of hope and hesitation. "Since our last meeting, things have improved. I feel... different. More capable."

Following Rob into his house, they followed Rob's gesture for them to sit down. The evening light filtered through the living room, casting long shadows across artefacts that whispered of forgotten voyages.

Sam noticed the subtle shift in Rob's posture, shoulders slightly less hunched, eyes carrying a glimmer of something new. Hope, perhaps. Or the first tentative steps toward healing.

"You look so different tonight," Sam remarked, his voice warm with genuine appreciation. "A confident mindset is a powerful thing. It allows you to release the negative aspects that hold you back."

Al watched carefully, reading the language of Rob's body. The way his hands moved. The set of his jaw. The almost imperceptible tremor suggested there was still deeper emotions lurking just beneath the surface.

Rob's laugh was soft, tinged with vulnerability. "It's because of you two," he admitted. "Our first meeting reminded me of who I used to be. Who I could be again." He paused, his fingers unconsciously tracing the edge of a nearby map. "But tonight feels different. Tonight, I feel like I'm standing at a crossroads."

Sam and Al exchanged knowing glances at each other. How this evening went could completely change Rob's life.

"I want to reveal everything," Rob continued, his voice dropping to almost a whisper. "But I'm terrified. There's so much pain. So much sorrow. What if sharing breaks me?"

Sam leaned forward, his movement deliberate. "Sharing doesn't break you," he said softly. "Silence does.

Rob's ocean blue eyes filled with a complexity of emotions. Fear battled with hope. Vulnerability wrestled with determination.

"The Cloak of Happiness," Sam said gently, redirecting their conversation. "What's beneath it, Rob?"

A heavy silence descended. Rob's massive frame seemed to fold in on itself, the confident exterior crumbling. His hands began to tremble almost unnoticeably.

"I'm afraid," Rob whispered, the admission hanging in the air like a fragile thing. "Afraid of the journey. Afraid of what revealing might mean for my mental health. There must be another way forward." He looked at Sam, a desperate hope in his eyes. "What do you think? Is there another path?"

Sam and Al exchanged a look. Not of concern. Not of judgment. But of profound understanding. This was more than a conversation. This was a rescue mission of the soul.

Sam's eyes glazed over with a reflection of love, not just compassionate, but illuminated from within. He leaned forward, his hands resting gently on his knees.

"Rob," he began, his voice gentle but resolute, "I need to share something with you. A vision God gave me."

Rob's massive frame tensed. Al remained perfectly still, a silent support.

"In this vision," Sam continued, "I saw you standing at the edge of a great cliff. Behind you was a ship, your life covered in years of accumulated barnacles, rust, and hidden pain. The Cloak of Happiness was wrapped around you like chains, not as a protection, but a burden."

Rob's breath caught in his throat.

"In the vision," Sam's voice grew softer, "I saw two paths. One where you continue hiding, the cloak growing heavier with each passing year. The other, a path of light, of healing. A path where you remove the cloak, face your fears, and allow yourself to be free."

Tears began to form in Rob's eyes. He didn't wipe them away.

"The vision showed me that your mental health, your very essence, is waiting to be liberated. The cloak you've been wearing, it's not protecting you. It's suffocating you. Every moment you keep it on, you're moving further from your true self."

Al watched carefully, he put his hand on Rob's shoulder. "Courage isn't the absence of fear," he added gently. "It's moving forward despite that fear."

"God showed me," Sam said, his voice now a whisper, "that your healing begins the moment you're willing to be vulnerable. To admit your pain. To lift up the cloak."

Rob's hands began to tremble. "I'm scared," he whispered.

Sam's response was immediate. "Fear is natural. But it doesn't define you. Your courage to face this moment that's what defines you."

The silence that followed was thick with possibility. "I want to be free," Rob finally said, the words barely audible.

Sam smiled. A smile that spoke of understanding, of compassion, of divine hope."Then let's begin," he said simply.... And in that moment, everything changed.

The room seemed to hold its breath as Rob approached the Cloak of Happiness. Sam and Al watched silently as he lifted the embroidered fabric with trembling hands. Carefully, and respectfully, Rob folded the cloak and placed it on a chair. The cloak had been covering a miniature church, not just a model, but a testament of love, of memory, of shared devotion.

Sam and Al looked on in amazement, their breath catching in their throats. The church was a masterpiece of expert craftsmanship. Delicate stained-glass windows caught the evening light, casting rainbow prisms across the room. Every minute detail spoke of precision, of love, of shared passion.

"It's extraordinary," Al whispered, his voice thick with emotion.

Rob's fingers traced the miniature church's spire, a gesture so tender it seemed to bridge past and present. "Anna and I," he began, his voice cracking, "we built this together." The story began to unfold like a delicate map of love and loss. "We were more than husband and wife," Rob continued. "We were partners. Best friends. Every piece of this church, we crafted together." A tear traced a path down his weathered cheek. "Our passion wasn't just in the building. It was in the worshipping. The serving."

Sam and Al sat perfectly still, creating a sacred space for Rob's memories.

"We were part of the worship congregation," Rob said, a hint of pride breaking through his grief. "Everywhere we went, we made friends. Connected with people. Loved unconditionally."

The miniature church seemed to pulse with the energy of Rob's shared memories. Each tiny window, each carefully carved wooden beam told a story of connection, of faith, of an unbreakable love.

"When Anna passed," his tone bearing his sadness, "it was like losing a part of myself. Two years of emptiness. Of silence."

Sam's hand moved, not quite touching Rob, but offering support.

"Tell us about Anna," he said softly.

Rob's eyes came alive. "My queen," he said, the term of endearment spoken with such reverence it seemed to fill the entire room. "We did everything together. Worshipped together. Served together. Loved together."

Sam leaned forward, his compassion poured from his heart.

"Grief is a journey," he said gently. "Not a destination. And you're not alone on this journey."

"I miss her," Rob whispered. "But I think... I think she would want me to live. To truly live."

Al's smile was gentle and understanding. "And what would living look like for you, Rob?"

"Returning to church," Rob said, a spark of hope igniting in his eyes. "The reconnecting. Worshipping again. Being part of a community."

Sam reached out, briefly touching Rob's hand. "Your love story with Anna isn't over," he said. "It's just... continuing in a different way."

"Thank you," Rob whispered, looking at the delicate model. "Thank you for helping me see."

Outside, the evening light began to soften, painting the room in hues of hope and possibility. The Cloak of Happiness lay folded, no longer a barrier but a memory. And Rob, for the first time in two years, began to breathe freely. He knew, deep in his soul, that his journey of healing had finally begun.

The evening settled around Aunty's house like a familiar embrace. Sam and Al entered, carrying with them the weight of Rob's story, a mixture of triumph, compassion, and spiritual revelation. Sam's steps were heavy, reflective. His slender frame seemed to carry the emotional burden of their recent encounter. Each movement spoke of a deep, internal processing, the way one might carry a precious, fragile memory. Al moved differently. Where Sam was contemplative, Al was steady. His movements were deliberate, purposeful. His eyes held a mixture of satisfaction and anticipation, like a sailor who had successfully navigated treacherous waters.

Aunty watched them enter, her keen eyes reading their body language like an open book. The kettle was already on, tea preparations beginning, her way of creating a sacred space for sharing.

"Well?" Coolness asked, her voice cutting through the evening silence. She stood by the window, her silhouette sharp against the fading light, tension coiled in her posture.

Sam dropped into his usual armchair, his hands running through his hair. "It was about love," he began, his voice soft. "About loss. About healing."

Al moved to help Aunty with the tea, his actions showing a silent gesture of appreciation.

"Rob's wife, Anna," Sam continued, "they were more than just partners. They were... a complete universe to each other."

Marg's knitting needles stilled. "Grief," she said softly, "can be the most profound love letter we never get to send."

Coolness turned from the window, her usually controlled demeanour showing a rare vulnerability. "Tell us everything," she urged.

And so, they did. Sam spoke of the miniature church, of how the Cloak of Happiness had been covering it for the past two years, and of Rob's journey through loss. Al would interject, adding depth, providing context, their storytelling delivered in perfect harmony.

Aunty listened, her hands moving methodically as she poured the tea. "You're leaving tomorrow," Marg said. It wasn't a question.

Sam's laugh was soft, tinged with both sadness and love. "The Canal path calls," he said. "Following the North Star. God's guidance."

Al nodded, adding, "Not an end. Just another beginning."

Coolness moved closer. "How do you do it?" she asked. "How do you keep going? Keep helping?"

Sam's response was immediate. "We don't," he said. "God does. We're just... vessels."

The room fell into a profound silence. Outside, the night began to settle, The North Star shone brightly creating a celestial path waiting to be followed.

Aunty sighed heavily. "One more night," she said, her tone a mixture of blessing and farewell. "One more night of sharing your stories."

Marg reached out, squeezing Sam's hand. "The Canal path," she said, her voice carrying a balance of wisdom. "Not everyone is called to walk it. But those who are, they carry something special."

Al's hand found Sam's shoulder, he squeezed it gently, showing his gratitute of their shared purpose.

"Tell us about the Canal path," Coolness urged, her curiosity overriding her usual reserve.

And as the night deepened, stories began to unfold. Stories of previous journeys. Of unexpected encounters. Of divine guidance manifesting in the most extraordinary ways. The house seemed to breathe with their narratives, as Aunty's living room became a sanctuary of spiritual revelations.

Sam looked at Al, a look that spoke volumes. Their journey was never about the destination. It was about the path, God's path. It was about listening. About being present.

"We go where we're needed," Sam said simply.

And in that percise moment, everyone understood that *'needed'* was a far more profound word than any geographical location.

The North Star awaited. God called. The Canal path was expecting them once again. And Sam and Al would answer, as they always had.

The morning light filtered through Aunty's kitchen, casting a soft glow on the faces of those about to part ways. Sam and Al stood near the doorway, their travel bags packed, the weight of countless journeys evident in their postures.

Aunty's eyes glistened with a mixture of pride and motherly concern. "You'll be careful?" she asked, her voice a blend of question and prayer.

Sam's smile was gentle, reassuring. "God guides our steps," he said softly. "He will keep us safe."

Coolness moved closer, giving Sam and Al a hug. Tears threatened to spill from her eyes, sighing she composed herself. "I'm sure Our Heavenly Father will bring you both back to us soon."

Al chuckled, a deep, warm sound. "So am I, He knows how much we love Aunty's cooking" he responded. "It's without doubt the best in the world."

Aunty pressed a small package into Sam's hands.

"Something for the journey," she said, her fingers lingering for a moment. "A bit of home to carry with you."

"Aunty," Sam said, his voice thick with emotion, "you didn't have to—"

"Hush," she interrupted, her eyes twinkling. "The best journeys are those shared, even when physically apart. Now let's all pray."

Aunty began the prayer, seeking God's protection, His blessing. Her hands, weathered by years of love and service, reached out to touch Sam and Al.

"May the North Star guide you," she said, her voice carrying the devotion of countless prayers. "And may you find those who need finding."

The goodbyes were a river of emotions, love, anticipation, and a profound sense of connection that transcended physical separation.

The November morning transformed the canal path into a crystalline wonderland. Frost adorned every surface like delicate lace, turning the landscape into a breathtaking canvas of winter's artistry. Bare branches sparkled with ice crystals, each twig a fragile sculpture catching the pale winter sunlight. The North Star hung tentatively in the grey sky, a faint but persistent guide, its light a subtle reminder of divine direction.

Sam and Al walked with the practiced rhythm of companions, their steps synchronized, their spirits attuned to something beyond the physical path before them.

"God is speaking," Sam murmured, his voice barely above a whisper.

Al nodded, understanding implicit in his silence.

The canal path stretched before them. Sam's steps became more deliberate, his body subtly shifting as if guided by an invisible hand. "Someone is coming," he said softly. The morning's sharp cold air, captured their breathes, creating delicate clouds that dissolved almost instantly.

In the distance, a figure began to take shape. At first, just a silhouette against the grey-white landscape. Then the figure emerged. A young Caribbean man, perhaps in his early twenties, walking with a mixture of purpose and hesitation. His hair styled in dreadlocks, a vibrant statement, woven with green, black, and gold, colours of heritage and hope. Each lock representing a cultural pride. He wore a heavy winter coat, dark blue with subtle patterns that seemed to shimmer slightly in the winter light. His boots were worn but carefully maintained, the kind of footwear that suggested journeys taken and challenges overcome.

Sam felt a surge of spiritual energy. The hairs on the back of his neck stood up, not from cold, but from something deeper. Something divine.

"Al," he whispered, "do you feel it?"

Al's response was a subtle nod. Their friendship allowed them to communicate beyond words.

The young man drew closer. His walk was deliberate, yet there was a clear vulnerability in his posture. Eyes that had seen too much for someone so young. A spirit both wounded and resilient.

Sam's heart began to race. This was more than a chance encounter. This was a divine appointment. The North Star seemed to pulse slightly in the grey sky, a celestial beacon guiding their path. "God," Sam breathed, "what is it that you are preparing Lord?"

The young man approached, carrying with him a story waiting to be told, a story waiting to be understood.

The man's dreadlocks seemed to dance with each step he took, "Hi, chaps," he greeted, his Caribbean accent carrying both urgency and reverence. "Are you the two men of God I'm looking for? I'm your servant, Adio."

Sam's eyes softened, recognizing the spiritual weight behind the young man's words. He patted the seat of a bench beside him, an invitation both physical and metaphorical. "Sit with us, Adio. Your name means 'righteous given by God,' doesn't it?"

A flicker of surprise crossed Adio's face.

"You know the meaning of my name?"

Al chuckled warmly. "God often prepares paths before we even understand them."

Adio settled beside them, his body tense with a mixture of hope and desperation. The frost-covered ground glimmered beneath their feet with silvery threads.

"My people," Adio began, his voice gaining strength, "we Jamaican men understand something profound about God. Through our suffering and beliefs in Jesus not being European, we will be saved. Black people have made a covenant with God. Our suffering, our struggle, it's all part of that divine covenant."

Sam leaned forward, his entire being present and ready to listen. "Tell us more, Adio" he encouraged softly.

Adio's hands began to move, painting pictures with his words. "Our identity is more than the chains of history. We are a people chosen, a people resilient. But now," his voice broke, "my mother is ill. Seriously ill."

Al sat listening carefully, "What's happening with your mother?" He asked, his tone revealed his compassion.

The young man's eyes filled with tears. Not of weakness, but of profound love and concern. "She's been the cornerstone of our family. A warrior of faith. But now she's battling an illness that seems to be consuming her. I've prayed. I've believed. But I need more than my own faith now."

Sam's response was immediate, born of countless encounters on their spiritual journey. "God's plan is never limited by our understanding," he said gently. "Tell us about her."

Adio's story began to unfold. His mother, a pillar of the community, had raised him and his sister single-handedly. A woman who had fought poverty, racism, and personal struggles, always holding onto her faith. She had taught her children that their identity was rooted in a divine promise, that their skin tone was not a curse, but a blessing.

"She needs more than medical healing," Adio whispered. "She needs a spiritual restoration."

Sam nodded, the glow of understanding flickered in his eyes. "And that's why you sought us out?"

"I believe God guided me to you," Adio said simply. "I have heard the stories. The ones of the two strangers on a canal path following the North Star to do God's work."

"Let's go to her," Sam said, standing. His movement was fluid and purposeful. "Your mother's needs are now our needs."

As they began to walk, Adio's relief was visible. "Thank you," he said, his voice a mixture of hope and vulnerability. "Our house is just a short walk from here."

The canal path continued, frost sparkling, winter's breath holding its secrets. Three souls, now united by something far greater than coincidence. United in the glory of God.

The house embraced them with warmth that transcended physical temperature. Aromas of home-cooked Caribbean cuisine filled the air, a rich scent of spices that spoke of love, tradition, and nurturing. Jerk chicken, rice, peas, and something that smelled like sweet plantains created a sense of comfort.

Adio's sister Tyonna stood in the doorway of the living room, her presence both welcoming and protective. The room was a statement of their family's journey, walls adorned with photographs capturing moments of joy, struggle, and resilience, each picture telling a story of love and perseverance.

"Welcome," she greeted, her voice carrying the same musical Caribbean cadence as her brother's. "I'm Tyonna. God has truly guided you here."

Sam noticed how her eyes, deep brown, intelligent, and perceptive seemed to look not just at them, but through them. Al's hand instinctively moved to Sam's shoulder, a gesture of kinship in this shared spiritual purpose.

"Tea," Tyonna announced, moving to the kitchen with practiced grace.

The kettle whistled its familiar song, and soon the most extraordinary tea materialized. Rich, dark, with hints of ginger and something Sam couldn't quite identify. Possibly nutmeg? Each cup was more than just a beverage, it was an offering of hospitality, of hope.

"Our mother," Adio said softly as they finished their tea, "she's been waiting for God to send someone. She's upstairs in her bedroom. For these past few weeks, she hasn't even had the strength to get up. We should go up to her now." The stairs creaked with history as they climbed each step. Family framed photographs lined the walls, generations of proud people of survival, of faith.

Taniyah's bedroom was a sanctuary of sorts. Soft light filtered through lace curtains, illuminating a woman whose spirit seemed larger than her physical body. Her eyes, sharp, intelligent, filled with an inner light, locked onto Sam and Al the moment they entered.

"I've been expecting you," she said, her voice soft but powerful. "God told me help would come."

Sam felt a shiver run down his spine. Not of fear, but of recognition.

Taniyah continued, "Three weeks I've been battling this chest infection. The doctor prescribed amoxicillin, but I'm scared. Why should I take these medicines?"

Sam leaned forward, his entire being radiating compassion. "Healing," he said gently, "comes in many forms. Sometimes through prayer. Sometimes through medicine. Often, through both."

Tyonna, who had followed them, stood in the doorway. Her hand rested on the doorframe, a silent guardian watching over her mother.

"Our mother," Adio explained, "she's a warrior. She's fought harder battles than this infection."

Taniyah's laugh was unexpected, rich, warm, and full of life. "Battles are won through faith," she said. "And sometimes, through listening."

Al's hand found Sam's shoulder, this was more than a medical intervention. This was a spiritual awakening.

"Tell us about your fears," Sam said softly. "About the antibiotics."

Taniyah's eyes filled with tears, not of weakness, but of deep, profound emotion. "I've seen medicines harm our community," she whispered. "Seen treatments that weren't meant to heal, but to control."

Adio stepped closer to his mother's bed. "But this is different, Mama," he said softly. "These are meant to help. To restore."

"God sends help in unexpected ways," Taniyah said, her gaze moving between Sam and Al. "But he always sends it."

Sam smiled a smile that spoke of understanding, of compassion. "We're here to hear you," he said simply. "Luke, who was the author of the Gospel of Luke, was more than just a writer," he explained, leaning closer to Taniyah. "He was a physician and historian. Jesus is known as the Great Physician. The Lord healed many people. Hezekiah's healing came from a cake of figs applied to his skin. My dear Taniyah, there is nothing to fear. We promise you. Please take your antibiotics, so you can get well."

Taniyah's fingers traced the medicine bottle. "I've been afraid," she whispered, her voice carrying decades of experiences, of mistrust and resilience. Her hand trembled slightly as she opened the bottle, but then her eyes burned with a newfound determination.

"The Lord," Sam murmured, "works through many channels. Through prayer. Through medicine. Through people." His eyes held a depth of understanding that transcended mere words.

A tear traced a path down Taniyah's cheek. Not of fear, but of release. "Tell me about Luke," she said softly.

Sam's smile was warm, and encouraging. "A Greek physician who became a devoted follower of Christ. He understood something profound about healing. He knew healing is not just physical. It's also spiritual."

Taniyah took the first tablet, her movements deliberate. As she swallowed, a transformation seemed to occur. Her shoulders straightened. Her eyes cleared.

"I feel it," she said, a broad smile breaking across her face. "Something is changing."

Adio and Tyonna, who had been standing in the doorway, exchanged a look of pure wonder. Weeks of worry seemed to melt away in that single moment. When they returned to the living room, Adio could barely contain his emotions. "We thought we were losing her," he said, his voice cracking. "For weeks, we've watched our mother fade. We've prayed. We've hoped. We felt so powerless."

Tyonna's hand found her brother's, squeezing gently. "You've done something miraculous," she said to Sam and Al. "Something we couldn't."

Sam's response was immediate, humble. "We're just vessels," he said softly. "God does the healing."

Al nodded, adding, "Sometimes healing requires someone from outside to see what those closest cannot."

Adio leaned forward, his entire being radiating gratitude and hope. "Please," he said, his Caribbean accent thick with emotion, "stay with us tonight. Break bread with our family. Let us show you our gratitude."

The invitation was more than a simple request for hospitality. It was a spiritual offering. A way of acknowledging the miracle they had just witnessed.

"We would be honoured," Sam said, understanding the profound significance of the moment.

Tyonna was already in the kitchen, her movements creating a promise of extraordinary Caribbean cuisine. Spices began to dance in the air, jerk chicken, rice and peas, plantains, each aroma telling a story of a true heritage.

"In our culture," Adio explained, "sharing a meal is more than just eating together. It is a communion, a connection of love."

Sam's smile was knowing. "Breaking bread together," he said, "is one of the most profound acts of spiritual fellowship."

As they prepared for the meal, the house seemed to pulse with renewed hope. The photographs of generations past looked upon them from the walls, silent witnesses to this moment of unexpected transformation. Adio watched his guests with a mixture of pride and anticipation. "This is my great-grandmother's recipe," he said, his voice carrying the weight of respect. "Every spice speaks of our culture."

Sam's first bite was a moment of pure revelation. His eyes closed involuntarily, savouring the complex layers of flavour. "It's like," he paused, searching for the right words, "like tasting a little bit of heaven."

Al laughed, a rich, warm sound that filled the room. "Heaven that dances on the tongue," he added.

Tyonna suddenly beamed with pride. "Mama taught me how to cook. She always says cooking is an act of love," she explained. "Each dish is a prayer."

The conversation flowed as freely as the food. Stories of family, of heritage, of survival, spoken between bites of jerk chicken and spoonful's of curry sauced rice.

When Sam and Al came downstairs for breakfast the next morning.They were delighted to see Taniyah sitting at the table, a vision of restored health. Gone was the frailty of yesterday, in its place, a vibrant energy that seemed to illuminate the entire room.

Sam's smile was full of wonder and appreciation. "Well, Taniyah," he said, "those antibiotics certainly worked quickly. Oh, ye of plentiful faith."

Taniyah's laugh was a revelation, rich, and full of life. "Faith," she said, "works in mysterious ways. Sometimes through prayer. Sometimes through medicine. Often through the love of family and unexpected friends. But always through God."

Adio reached out, squeezing his mother's hand. The gesture spoke volumes, of gratitude, love, and relief.

The morning light filtered through the kitchen window, casting a soft glow on their faces. The North Star, though fading with the morning light, seemed to have guided them to this moment of profound restoration.

Taniyah looked around the table at her children, and at Sam and Al, these unexpected messengers of hope. "God," she said simply, "works in the most mysterious of ways."

And in that moment, everything felt possible...